love at the library

By Amanda Kai

Regal Swan Publishing

Copyright © 2020 Amanda Kai.

All rights reserved. No part of this publication may be reproduced, distributed, or transmitted in any form or by any means, including photocopying, recording, or other electronic or mechanical methods, without the prior written permission of the publisher, except in the case of brief quotations embodied in critical reviews and certain other noncommercial uses permitted by copyright law.
Front cover image by Emily Wittig.
First printing edition 2020. Regal Swan Publishing.

Chapter 1

The sun had just disappeared below the horizon when Megan Vasquez finished her shift at the coffee shop where she worked. The twenty-four-year-old traded her apron for her favorite purple hoodie and clocked out on the timesheet hanging in the back room. "Bye, Duke!" she called to her manager, a cheerful, pot-bellied man with dark skin and graying hair who Megan guessed to be in his early fifties.
"Take care of yourself, Megan! See you tomorrow!" Duke waved to her as she headed out the door. Duke would keep the Enchanted Moon coffee shop going for the late evening shift, finally closing up shop around ten. Until then, the hipsters and college students that frequented the Rosedale neighborhood's most popular hangout would continue to sip artisanal caffeinated beverages, endlessly clacking away on their laptops.

Megan shivered in the windy autumn air and pulled her hoodie over her brown wavy hair to keep warm. It was a long walk back to her apartment, about 20 blocks away. She wished that she could afford a car, or even a bicycle, to make the trip quicker. Sometimes she took public transportation, but the busses on her route between work and home ran infrequently, and they were often late. She had just missed the last bus, and it would be another hour before the next one came-- too long to wait around in the cold. She wished the City of Austin would improve their public transportation system.

Overhead, thunder rumbled, and the wind began to whip. Megan tried to take a shortcut through the neighborhood streets to get home faster. She hoped she could make it back before the rain came down. No such luck. She only made it one more block before the heavens opened and great drops came tumbling down onto her, soaking through her favorite purple hoodie. She needed to get her dad to send over her winter coat before she froze to death. Wasn't Texas supposed to be hot all the time?

She ducked under the nearest building that had an awning to try to escape, but the driving wind sent the torrents of rain at her in an almost-horizontal fashion. Megan began scanning the area for a better place of refuge. A few little retail stores, and some restaurants, lined Burnet Road. But with no money to spare, Megan knew she would just be loitering to kill time. Besides, she had just bought groceries to stock up her fridge and pantry. It would be a waste of money dining out, even just for a snack, when she knew there would be food waiting for her at home. Then she spotted a circular driveway leading off towards an old concrete building, set some distance from the main road on a side avenue. In the growing darkness she could just make out the sign: "Yarborough Library." What luck! Her pace quickened as she made her way across the driveway. She hurried up the slippery steps and inside, trying to shake the wetness off her shoes and clothes.

A buxom woman with skin like ebony sat at the front desk. "We close in thirty minutes," the woman informed Megan as she passed by.
"That's OK," Megan told her, "I just needed to get out of the rain for a bit."
In truth, she couldn't have picked a better place to wait out the storm. Libraries had been her place of refuge for as long as she could remember-- though not necessarily from an actual storm! Megan loved books. Her favorite childhood memories were of her mom reading Curious George and Madeline stories to her before she drifted off to sleep. As soon as Megan learned to read for herself, she would read any book she could get her hands on. Her mom and dad didn't have much money for books, so her mom would take her to the local library, where every week she could fill up a big canvas bag--or two-- of new stories to devour. But the library itself became a place of solace. As financial troubles piled higher, the fights and arguments between her parents grew louder and more frequent. Megan didn't want to go home after school, where the tension was high, and the shouting made it impossible to enjoy her books or do her homework. So, Megan began stopping by the library on her way home from school every day. She would get her homework done first, then curl up with a book or two for the next few hours. Sometimes, if the book was really good, she would even skip dinner to finish it. There was a big old armchair in the corner of the library by the art history books, made of the ugliest green upholstery you ever saw, and which bore some permanent brown stains on it. But Megan loved that chair. She sat in it so much that the librarians began calling it "Megan's chair" and kindly asking patrons to move from it if they knew it was almost time for school to let out. Megan missed that library. She hadn't been back since before college.

This library was old too, maybe built around the same decade as the one in her hometown of Santa Fe. Photographs on the walls showed that at one time, the building had been home to a movie theatre back in the 1960's, then later converted to a library. It gave her a sense of comfort to be there, surrounded by shelves of books. Plus, it was a place she knew she could go that was free; nobody would expect her to buy something or glare at her for gasping at any price tags. She wandered over to the fiction section, looking for one of her favorite authors. She thumbed through all the A's but didn't find what she was seeking. She checked some of the other shelves, thinking perhaps they organized things a little differently than other libraries, but still no luck. A search on the library's computer showed they had several copies of titles by this author, so she jotted down the call number of her favorite one, then returned to the section where it ought to be. Nope, not there.

Puzzled, she left the aisle. A young man with fair skin and glasses came around the corner pushing a cart full of books. He noticed the confused expression on Megan's face and stopped his cart. "Can I help you find something, ma'am?" he asked.

"Yes, actually. I'm looking for Jane Austen's *Pride and Prejudice*, but I can't seem to find any of her books."

A smile creased the corners of his mouth. "Ah, there's a reason for that. We've moved all of the Jane Austen books to a special display this month, in honor of the author's birthday." He shoved the cart off to the side and led Megan to a circular display in the middle of the room with a big sign. All of Jane's books were arranged on the feature, as well as some by similar authors from that time period.

"Here you go," the man handed her a volume of *Pride and Prejudice*. "I think this is what you were looking for, right?"

"Yes," Megan blushed. "I must be blind. I walked right past this display on my way to the fiction section and didn't even see it."

"That's OK." He absently raked his hand through his chestnut hair, making pieces of it stick up in the back. "So, uh, you're an Austen fan, huh?"

"Yeah," Megan nodded. "I've read all her books. I even read the unfinished ones, and the juvenilia."

"Wow. I don't think I've ever read any of hers."

"You're kidding! Not even in school?"

"Nope." He shook his head. "Our English lit teacher in High School must not have been a fan of hers; it wasn't required reading. He had us reading Tolstoy, Hugo, Wilde, Dickens, and plenty of others. Austen was on a list of optional reading, along with Trollope and the Bronte sisters, among others. I recall I ended up picking Shelley's *Frankenstein* off of that list. I think my fourteen-year old self thought that reading about a monster that comes to life sounded a lot more interesting than a romance book."

"I can't say I blame you," Megan shrugged.

"I'm Levi, by the way," he stuck out a hand.

"Megan," she returned the handshake.

"Pleased to meet you."

"Likewise."

"Well, uh, I'll let you enjoy your book, Megan," Levi said, "but let me know if there's anything else I can help you with."

She beamed back at him. "Thanks!"

As Megan wandered towards an upholstered sofa in the corner, she watched Levi return to his cart and begin reshelving the books. *He's kinda cute*, she thought, *and nice*. She shook her head to dismiss this train of thought. *You just got a new job, Megan,* she told herself, *you don't have time or money to be thinking about anything else right now. Besides, it's too soon…*

Megan had been lost in the world of Elizabeth Bennet and Mr. Darcy for about twenty minutes when the grumbling of her stomach brought her back to reality. She checked the window outside. The rain had let up, it seemed. *Time to head home,* she decided. She went to return the volume to its display and noticed Levi watching her.

"You can check that out, if you want to," he offered.

Megan fumbled with the book, trying to get it back onto the little metal book stand where it had been. "Oh, um, I don't have a library card."

"I can help you get one."

She shook her head. "I don't have a state driver's license or proof of residence with me."

"Not even an ID card?"

"I mean, I have my old driver's license from New Mexico. It works to get me into a club or buy a beer, if I want, but I can't drive or get registered for anything."

"You're not from around here, then, huh?" Levi's eyebrow shot up.

Megan bit her lip. "I moved to Austin a few months ago, but I only just got my own apartment last week. I don't have any utility bills to prove my address yet, and I don't have a car, so I haven't bothered to go to the DMV to update my license."

Levi nodded. "Understandable." He motioned for Megan to follow him to the front desk.

Leaning over towards the woman at the desk, he asked, "Hey, Loretta, do we have any of those little postcard thingies?"

"You mean the blank ones that patrons can use for change of address?" She reached under the counter and pulled out a card.

"That's the one." Turning to Megan he handed her the card and pen. "Fill this out, please."

Megan did as she was asked, then returned it to Levi.

"Thank you, Ma'am." With the card still in hand, he walked out the front door, leaving Megan bewildered.

"Mail's here," Levi announced as he waltzed back in. He went to the incoming mail slot and retrieved the postcard from the box attached to the wall.

"Is he always like this?" Megan whispered to Loretta.

"Honey, I've learned it's best not to ask," Loretta nodded in a hushed voice.

"Well, Ms. Megan," Levi grinned as he returned to the two ladies at the counter. "We have received mail from you with your address on it. We can now offer you a library card so that you can check out up to fifty books, four CDs, and two videos at a time."

Megan chuckled as a flush stole across her cheeks. "Just this one, for today, I think."

"Absolutely. Loretta, can you help Megan to check out her book?"

"Sure thing, Honey," the robust woman answered in her typical Southern fashion.

It was one thing that Megan still hadn't gotten used to. In New Mexico, most people reserved nicknames of that sort for their significant other. Since coming to Texas, she had been called "Honey," "Sweetie," "Darlin'," and a host of other sugary terms by perfect strangers, usually women. She found it very odd, until she realized they applied the terms to practically everybody they saw.

Loretta scanned *Pride and Prejudice* for her. "You're all checked out, Honey!"

"Thanks!" Megan beamed.

Megan looked forward to re-reading her favorite book, much like she would enjoy a visit with an old friend. She tucked the book carefully inside her hoodie in case the rain started to pour again, thanked Levi and Loretta again for all their help, and headed for home. Luckily, the weather held out and she made it back to her tiny third-floor apartment without incident.

Megan's stomach was threatening to eat her from the inside out if she didn't feed it, so the first thing she did was throw a pot of water on the stove and crack open a packet of ramen noodles into a bowl. A few carefully portioned squares of tofu were cut from the container in the fridge, for added protein, then she stirred the boiling water in and waited for the noodles to soften. She fingered the lettering on the cover of *Pride and Prejudice*, which sat on the table where she had deposited it after shedding her hoodie. It made her think about Levi. The way his short hair had stood on end when he ran his hand through it. The endearing smile that lit up his face. The horn-rimmed glasses that made him appear bookish, but not too nerdy. The brilliant blue eyes behind those glasses. *Stop it, Megan!* She chided herself. She shoved a big bite of ramen in her mouth, burning her tongue in the process. "Ow!" she said out loud.

Just then, her cell phone rang.

"Hey, *Chica*, whassup?" It was her best friend, Sierra.

"Nothin' much. Just eating some ramen."

"Ramen? I can feed you better than that. Listen, me and Patrice are about to get some grub over at Kerbey Lane. You wanna join us?"

"That's OK, I'm fine. I just got back home from work." Megan knew if she went out her friends would want to treat her. She hated always being the "broke girl" who was never able to treat them in return.

"This late?" The cresting intonation in Sierra's voice showed her surprise. "Duke didn't make you work overtime, did he?"

"Naw, I got stuck in the rain, but don't worry, I took shelter at this cool library I found."

"Ha, leave it to you to get stranded in your favorite place in the world-- somewhere loaded with books."

Megan laughed at Sierra's remark. "Yeah."
Sierra knew Megan well-- since High School. Sierra had been popular and on the cheerleading team, and Megan was the quiet one who always had a book at hand. Yet somehow, the two had hit it off and their friendship had stuck. Sierra had moved to Austin a year before Megan did, to go to grad school, and Megan was glad to be living in the same city with her again. Especially after Brad...
She didn't tell her friend about meeting Levi. Sierra would jump all over her if she heard she'd met somebody. Sierra had been trying for weeks to set her up with somebody new, but Megan was resistant. *The person who's the rebound always gets hurt.*
"You sure you don't wanna come out?" Sierra asked again. "I'm gonna order the Kerbey Queso. You know I can never finish that by myself, and Patrice is lactose intolerant."
"Naw, I'm good. I'm sure you can take home the leftovers."
"Okaay...well, if you're not gonna meet up with us, then we should definitely hang out this weekend."
"Yeah, for sure!" Megan answered.
"Oops, our table's ready, gotta go! Talk to you soon. *Besitos!*" Sierra made affectionate kissing sounds.
"*Muah, muah*! You too! Bye!" Megan returned the kisses before hanging up.
Megan turned back to her now-cold ramen. The noodles tasted soggy and mushy. She took the bowl to the microwave to reheat it and see if it could be salvaged. She would eat it anyways, even if it couldn't. Luckily, the modern technology put enough life back into her soup to make it palatable.
Too bad she couldn't reheat her life as easily as she could reheat her dinner, she thought.

Chapter 2

The next few days were so busy, Megan didn't have time to return to the library. One of the other employees at Enchanted Moon was out with the flu, so when Duke offered Megan some extra shifts to cover for him, she didn't hesitate to accept. The additional hours left her exhausted, but she knew she needed the money. When she wasn't on duty Megan spent her time submitting her resume online to various postings in data analysis-- which is the field her degree and former job were in. The job at Enchanted Moon was supposed to be temporary, just until she could get hired someplace else. It wasn't ideal, but it was all she could get right off the bat, and it paid the bills-- even if just barely.

Sierra called again on Saturday and invited Megan to go with her the next day to the Blanton Art Museum. She wanted to see the Andy Warhol exhibit they were showing. Sierra was studying art history at the University of Texas, so she liked to go whenever they had anything new on display. Sierra had an annual pass to the Blanton that let her bring a guest whenever she wanted, otherwise Megan probably would have declined on the basis of the cost. She tried to only do free outings whenever possible.

Sunday afternoon, Megan dressed comfortably in a pair of jeans, a long-sleeve t-shirt, and a sweatshirt that hid her curves and provided extra warmth. It wasn't that she thought of herself as fat, but she hated her love handles and the little muffin top that hung over her jeans and made her feel pudgy, especially since she was shorter than the average girl. She twisted her wavy hair into a messy bun and secured it with a hairband and a few bobby pins, letting a few brown strands dangle down. She smoothed out her beige skin with a layer of foundation and put on clear lip gloss to soften her dry lips. The weather forecast said it might be chilly later, so she grabbed her purple hoodie to layer on top of the sweatshirt and tee, in case she needed it. Megan made a mental note to call her dad that night and ask him to mail her winter coat from Santa Fe. She would need it if they had a big cold front. For now, these fall layers would have to do.

Megan took the bus to get downtown where the museum was. Sierra lived in West Campus just a few blocks from the Blanton, so for her it was easier to simply walk there. Megan sat on the front steps of the large modern edifice to wait. It wasn't long before she spotted her gorgeous friend. Sierra Ramón stood out in any crowd. Tall and willowy, with wavy brunette hair, a pointed nose, and flawless skin that sometimes made Megan envious. Sierra and Megan both had mixed parentage, but Sierra's features were whiter, while Megan's darker complexion made her look more Mexican. As a result, Sierra had an easier time fitting in with the popular crowd, whereas Megan often felt like she was never truly accepted by them.

"*Chica*!" Sierra bent down to give Megan a big squeeze. "How's it hanging, girl?"
"Whew, it's been a long week, I can tell you that much! Keenan went home with the flu on Tuesday, so I've been picking up some of his shifts."
"You're kidding! Wasn't he just sick with a cold or something the week before last? And out with something else a few days before that? I'll bet you anything he's just faking to get time off to be with that stupid girlfriend of his-- what's-her-face."
"Yep. Veronica," Megan filled in the name of Keenan's girlfriend. Megan had only met her twice in the few weeks since she'd started her job, but it seemed like she wasn't the best influence on Keenan.
"But he's the boss' nephew, so he's not likely to get sacked," she said. "In the meantime, I get to roll in the extra moola during his absence." Megan gestured by rubbing her thumb against her other fingers.
Sierra gasped. "Does that mean we can go out for Amy's Ice Cream after the museum later?"
Megan bit her lip. Sierra just rolled her eyes. "C'mon, let's go see the Warhol exhibit. I gotta take notes for Professor Yoshida's class and make some sketches. I'm doing a paper on pop art for my finals this semester."

The Warhol display was interesting. Megan had never been a big fan of pop art, but Sierra had been studying the movement in her classes lately, and she had plenty to say about the pieces being exhibited, which made it a lot more fun for Megan. Personally, Megan preferred older painting styles such as Rococo and Neoclassicism. After they finished in the Warhol exhibit, Megan wandered around to some of the other galleries, looking for paintings that suited her tastes more. As she turned the corner into the Impressionist wing, to her surprise, there was Levi! They made eye contact and he approached her.
He seemed equally amazed and pleased to see her again. "Fancy meeting you here!" his warm smile lit up the whole gallery and sent a flurry of butterflies into Megan's stomach. She tried not to stare at him. He must have been wearing contacts instead of his glasses, and his blue eyes looked even more dazzling in the light streaming at an angle through the gallery skylights.
A giggle escaped her lips, though she tried to bite them to contain it. "Same to you, I suppose. I took you for a book guy, not an art guy."
"A guy can have multiple interests, can't he? It's what I'd assume about you. You can't be all *Pride and Prejudice* and look down on every other pursuit in life." Another laugh left her mouth before she could stop it. This one louder and unmistakable.
"What's so funny?" Levi asked.

"Sorry! It's just that you said 'pride' and 'prejudice' like it was my character traits."

Levi laughed with her. "I guess I see what you mean. I didn't mean to put it that way, I'm sorry."

"No, it's fine!" Megan waved him off.

Sierra caught up with them. "Um, hi..." she stood awkwardly beside Megan.

"Oh, Sierra, I'm sorry. This is Levi. Levi, this is my best friend, Sierra Ramón. Levi and I met the other day at the library when I got caught in the rain there."

A sudden grin of realization spread across Sierra's face. She grabbed Levi's hand and shook it vigorously. "Levi, so nice to meet you!"

"Likewise."

"Are you here by yourself?"

"Yes, actually. I like to come here sometimes on my days off. I'm surrounded by books all day, so for a change of scenery, I like to be surrounded by art."

"A terrific philosophy! Don't you agree, Megan?" Sierra prodded.

"Um, yeah, it's great," Megan stammered.

"Since you're all alone, why don't you join us for the rest of our tour?" Sierra invited.

"Sure!" Levi accepted. "I can show you my favorite exhibit. It's just down this hall." Levi gestured the way.

"What about the impressionists?" Megan whispered to Sierra, who quickly waved her off.

"I can bring you back another day for them."

"What's that?" Levi asked, turning back around. "Have we missed an important part of the museum you wanted to see?"

Megan's cheeks turned pink. "It's nothing, really."

Levi smacked his forehead. "Of course! You were just entering this wing when I came out. We have to go back. You need to see the Bartholomé that's on loan here right now." Without a second thought, Levi grabbed Megan's hand and led her into the impressionist wing. Sierra followed at a distance, a sly grin all over her face.

Levi stopped in front of a painting by Albert Bartholomé labeled "The Artist's Wife." The pastels and charcoal depicted a lovely Victorian woman reclining while she read.

"She reminds me of you," Levi pointed.

"What?" Megan smiled.

"Reading your *Pride and Prejudice* book."

Megan laughed. "I do read other books, you know."

"Oh, I know. *Emma, Mansfield Park, Sense and Sensibility, Persuasion,*" Levi began rattling off the names he remembered from setting up the display in the library. More peals of laughter rung from Megan's lips. "I mean, I read other authors too!"

"Who else do you enjoy?" Levi asked as they began strolling to look at other paintings.

"Charlotte Bronte, L.M. Montgomery, Laura Ingalls Wilder, Francis Hodgson Burnett, to name a few."

"So just dead women," Levi quipped.

Megan was a little taken aback. "No... I like C.S. Lewis and J.R.R. Tolkien too."

"Getting better. We've added some dead men to the list."

Megan didn't know what to say in response.

Levi grinned back at her. "Don't worry, I like Lewis and Tolkien too! When it comes to fantasy, they're the gold standard in my book."

"I couldn't have said it better myself," Megan agreed.

"Do you read a lot of fantasy and sci-fi?"

"A little. I tend to hover on the classics."

"I noticed."

"Who do you like to read?" Megan asked him.

"Neil Gaiman. Terry Pratchett. A lot of indie authors, actually. Andy Weir, Lindsay Buroker, Jeff VanderMeer, China Mieville."

"Neat!" Megan had heard of Gaiman and Pratchett, but the indie ones were unknown to her.

They finished looking through all the artwork in the impressionist gallery, talking the whole while about books they had read recently. Megan got so caught up in their conversation, it wasn't until they reached the end of the hallway and she glanced behind her that she realized Sierra was no longer keeping up with them.

"Over here is the exhibition I wanted to show you," Levi began heading towards the next area.

Megan grabbed his arm gently. "Hang on, we need to wait for Sierra to catch up with us."

Sierra was on her cell phone but seeing that the others were waiting ahead of her, she trotted to catch up to them. She got off the call just as she reached them.

"Did you get to finish looking at everything in the impressionist wing?" Megan asked.

Sierra waved her hand. "Oh, I saw everything that I needed to see. I can come back anytime with my membership, remember? Anyways, I forgot that I promised Patrice I would help her study for our final with Professor Yoshida next week, so I gotta run. You don't mind showing her the rest of the museum, do you, Levi?"

"Not at all!" he grinned.

"But you said you wanted to go for Amy's after this," Megan protested.

"Maybe next time we can grab an ice cream together," Sierra apologized. "It'll be my treat then," she said to make up for it. "Bye, *Chica*! Enjoy the rest of the exhibits." Sierra gave Megan a quick squeeze, then she was off.

"Shall we?" Levi gestured to the next gallery. Megan nodded, chewing her lip to hide her embarrassment. She had a feeling that Sierra had never promised anything to Patrice and was just using the phone call as an excuse to push her into a blind date with Levi.

They entered a spacious modern room with a high ceiling and skylight windows. It resembled the last gallery they were in. But what struck Megan were the long scrolls painted with what appeared to be Chinese writing suspended from the rafters. More scrolls were hung in panels lining the two longest sides of the room. In the center of the room covering most of the floor, row upon row of hand-printed books were laid open upon a low platform, as if begging to be read, and at one end of the room, highly decorated books that looked like valuable ancient texts were displayed on another platform, like a holy altar that only a priest ought to touch. For a bibliophile like Megan, such an artistic display of books and writing moved her to the point she could not even speak at first. She just wandered the room apart from Levi, admiring all the texts.

Finally, she asked, "are all of these real books?"

Levi shook his head. "The artist, Xu Bing, created all of these himself. He even made up the characters that are printed; it's not real Chinese, just pseudo-Chinese. Nobody can read them, not even him."

Megan frowned. "Why make books that nobody can read?"

"That's part of the art, I guess. Part of the mystery. It's called 'Book from the Sky', but it's written in a language that doesn't exist on Earth."

"Like a message sent down from Heaven," Megan gasped. "Written in a language no man can speak."

Levi smiled. "That's beautiful." He scratched his hair, making it stick up again. "It's better than what I thought about it."

"Yeah? What did you think?"

"I kept thinking about how irritating it would be to find a book and try to read it, only to discover it's not in any language I can understand."

Megan laughed. "Yeah, I can see how that would be very frustrating."

They looked at some of the other museum exhibits for another half hour, until Megan's stomach rumbled loudly.

"Are you hungry?" Levi asked.

Put on the spot, Megan tried to deny it. "I'm fine, really." She began chewing her lip again.

"You mentioned wanting ice cream earlier. Wanna go with me to get some Amy's?"

"I... don't have a car. I'd have to take the bus and meet you there." She didn't know why her lack of transportation made her feel embarrassed.

"I have a car," Levi offered. "You can ride with me, if you'd like."

Megan thought about it for a moment. Levi was still basically a stranger to her. What if he was a wolf in sheep's clothing? She'd heard horrible stories about women who accepted rides from strangers, only to disappear without a trace--

or worse. She was unconsciously gnawing her lip so hard that it began to bleed. The metallic taste awakened her senses. If Sierra were here, she would tell Megan to just 'go with him', not to worry about whether Levi was a good person or not. To trust her instincts.
"Well? Shall we?" Levi repeated his invitation.
"Uh, yeah," Megan weakly replied. "I guess some ice cream wouldn't hurt."
"I'll make sure we don't go overboard and spoil our dinner," Levi winked. *Was that a dinner invitation as well?* Megan didn't know.

They got to Amy's Ice Cream, and Megan ordered her usual-- Mexican Vanilla. She didn't know why she liked something so simple, but for whatever reason, the creamy taste of the vanilla just suited her taste buds. Levi, however, was interested in trying the flavor of the month, "Booger Monster." Any ice cream with a name like that sounded absolutely disgusting to Megan. She watched the employee make it for him to see what exactly was in it. It turned out the base was their butter ice cream, flavored with creme de menthe and peppermint, and chocolate chips and marshmallows crushed in.

They paid for their ice cream and sat down to eat their treats.
"So, tell me about yourself. Where are you from? What do you do?" Levi inquired.
Megan felt her cheeks grow warm again. She really hated being put on the spot.
"Well, I grew up in Santa Fe. My dad still lives there, actually. I got my degree in data analytics from the University of New Mexico--"
"That's in Albuquerque, right?" Levi interrupted.
"--right. Then I got hired by a big tech company in Santa Fe after I graduated so I moved back there."
"What brought you to Austin, then?"
Megan hesitated. She wasn't sure she was ready to tell her whole story, just yet. So, she told just part of it. "I got an offer for a startup company that was here, so I took it."
"Is that where you work now?"
"No. I moved all the way out here, but then it turned out that the company wasn't doing well. They lost some of their investors. So, then they couldn't afford to keep me. I had been there less than a month. Last one in, first one out."
"Couldn't your old company take you back?"
"I tried asking, but unfortunately, they had already filled my position. Plus, I used up all my savings to get out here. I can't afford to move back right away."
"So, what are you doing right now?"
"I took the first job I could find, as a barista for the Enchanted Moon coffee shop. It's not great, but it will keep me afloat until I can get something better. But enough about me," Megan shook her head. "What about you? I know nothing about you, except that you work at the library."
A laugh erupted from Levi's mouth. "Well, let's see. I grew up in a little town

outside of Houston where my parents own a coffee shop. Went to UT Austin, art major."

"That explains why you liked the Blanton so much."

Levi nodded. "But, as it turns out, I don't have very much talent for art. I dropped out in my junior year. Didn't know what I would do with myself. I've always loved books, always found the library to be something like my second home," Levi explained. Megan could relate to that. "So, when I saw that they had an opening for a library assistant, I took it. That was almost a year ago."

"Have you thought about going back to school? Finishing your degree and getting a master's in library science?"

"Yep. Thought about it. Trouble is, I would have to figure out what to get my basic degree in. Art didn't pan out."

"Maybe English Lit?" Megan suggested.

Levi shrugged. "Maybe. But like I said, I've never been real big on the classics. Sci-fi, fantasy, horror, even comics. That's my stride."

Megan had finished her tiny cup of ice cream by now, and her stomach was still growling.

"Want some of mine?" Levi offered the big cup of Booger Monster to her. She looked at it dubiously.

"I promise, there are no actual boogers in here!"

His comment made Megan snort. She took another look at the mashup of mint and marshmallows. It did look tempting. "OK, I'll try it. Using her spoon, she took a heaping bite from his cup. The minty flavor made her tongue tingle and the marshmallows warmed up the ice cream just enough to keep the huge bite from giving her a brain-freeze.

"Mmm, that's good!" she exclaimed.

"I'm full already. You can have the rest if you want," he offered.

Megan devoured the remainder of Levi's ice cream.

"Where do you live? I'll take you home," he said as they got back into his car. Once again, Megan's trust issues sent her emotions into warning mode.

"Oh, um, I'm close enough to walk from the library. You can just take me there."

"Okay," Levi agreed. "My shift is going to start soon anyways."

They pulled into the parking lot at Yarborough library. Megan fumbled to find her purse, which had slid to the floor of the car. In the meantime, Levi raced around the car to open the door for her and held his hand out to help her out. His brash chivalry made Megan laugh. "I'm capable of opening my own car door," she said.

"I know. I just wanted to, that's all."

"Thank you," she said as she took his hand to exit the vehicle. "Here, I thought chivalry had died along with men like Mr. Darcy."

"Mr. Darcy? Who's he?"

"The hero of *Pride and Prejudice*. Trust me, he's the one that all women model their ideal man after. Unfortunately, men like him don't seem to exist anymore.

Although, you seem to be doing a good job of giving him a run for his 10,000 pounds a year," Megan told him.

"Is that all he makes?" Levi's eyebrows went up.

"In those days, it was like being a billionaire."

"Wow, so he's super rich, and super chivalrous. Is he handsome too?"

"Oh, without a doubt!"

Levi grinned. "Gee, how can a guy like me even hope to compete with a fictional character like that?"

Megan laughed again. She followed Levi into the library. As they passed through the security tag detectors at the entrance, an idea sparked in her mind.

"Did you know there's a zombie apocalypse version of *Pride and Prejudice*?"

"You're kidding!"

"Not at all! In this variation, sometime before the novel, there was a plague brought to Europe from the West Indies that turned a bunch of people into zombies. Everyone has to learn how to fight them, so they study Chinese and Japanese martial arts. The story is basically the original text of *Pride and Prejudice*, but there are extra scenes thrown in where they have to fight the zombies that are attacking everywhere. Like, they're in the middle of a ball, then all of a sudden, there's a zombie that shows up and the heroes and heroines whip out their swords and daggers to fight back."

"Cool!" Levi was intrigued. "Let's see if the library has it."

Sure enough, there was a copy of *Pride and Prejudice and Zombies* on the shelf in the fiction section.

"I didn't even know anyone wrote any spin-offs of Jane Austen's novels."

"Oh, sure!" Megan nodded. "There are actually a lot of authors who write stories based on her books. Quite a few of them have even been published."

"Really? I thought fanfiction was stuck in the realm of internet-based freebie stories, usually with bad writing."

"Some are, for sure. There have been some pretty bad ones, I'll admit. But there are also a lot of great Jane Austen fanfiction stories out there." She named several of her favorite authors who wrote Jane Austen variations and told about some of the plot twists. Some wrote sequels to the books, she said. Others wrote versions of the story where something different happens, like what if Mr. Darcy and Elizabeth had met earlier, or in a different setting. Some gave *Pride and Prejudice* a whole different spin, like making Mr. Darcy a vampire, or a pirate, or a prince.

"Well, I guess I'd have to read the original first, to really appreciate it. But, if you say this one is good, I'll start here," he held up the *Zombies* version.

"I hope you enjoy it!" Megan smiled.

A middle-aged man with a receding hairline was working the checkout counter.

"Nice to see you have a new friend, Levi!" he remarked.

"Oh, hey, this is my friend, Megan," Levi introduced. "Megan, this is our head librarian, Bartholomew."

"Please, call me 'Bart'," the man smiled, extending his hand to Megan. He helped Levi check out *Pride and Prejudice and Zombies*.

"Hey, I almost forgot," Levi called as Megan turned to go home. "I never got your phone number."
"Oh, uh, sure," Megan mumbled. She rattled off the number to him, while he punched the digits into his phone's address book. "Well, I've gotta get going now," she said, chewing her lip again. Levi was still typing on the phone. Suddenly, her own phone dinged.
"I sent you a text message," Levi explained. "Now you'll have my number too."
"Thanks!" Megan smiled.
"Have a good night, Megan," Levi waved.
"You too!"

While Megan was walking home, she pulled her phone out to read the text from Levi.
Thanks for inviting me to accompany you at the museum and going to get ice cream with me. I had a really great time. Here's my number.
Hope to see you again sometime soon.
-Levi Whittaker

Megan smiled. She hoped to see Levi again soon too.

Chapter 3

The weather was getting chilly now that the sun was down as Megan walked from the library back to her apartment. The layers she had put on that afternoon were no longer warm enough to keep out the wind. Megan hadn't checked the weather forecast, but she guessed this might be a cold front coming in. Sure enough, when she opened her weather app, it showed a sharp drop in temperature over the next few hours. Darn it! Why hadn't she planned better and gotten home sooner? Megan cursed to herself.

As soon as she got in the door, she put the teakettle on, then called her dad. Gabriel Vasquez answered on the third ring.
"Hey, *Mija*, what's up?" he asked.
"Oh, nothing much, Dad," she replied. "How are you doing?"
"I'm fine, same as always," her dad said. "What about you? Anything interesting happening there in the capital of the Lone Star State?"
"Hehe, just the usual. Work. Friends. Reading books," Megan tittered. "I do have a favor to ask, though."
"Anything for you, sweetie!"
"Could you send me my winter coat? The big puffy one with the fur collar on it? I think it's hanging in my bedroom closet"
"Didn't think that winters could get that cold in Texas, huh?" Gabriel quipped.
"Sierra kept complaining when she moved out here that it was 'hotter than Hell'. And when I got here, it was August, and she didn't seem to be in the wrong."
"I still don't get why you gave up a great job to follow that no-good loser of a boyfriend out there. And then he had to go and cheat on--"
"-- I really don't want to talk about that, Dad," Megan interrupted him. "At least Sierra and Patrice let me crash at their place until I could get my own apartment."
"Yeah," her dad said, resigned. He changed the subject. "Is the apartment nice?"
Megan looked around the tiny studio. The brick exterior wall was crumbling in places and the light fixture above her flickered. The place was old, dilapidated, but it was all she could afford.
"It's great, Dad!" She lied, trying to be cheery. "Just a cozy little nook the right size for me." The apartment did have one great feature, the bay window seat which overlooked the park across the street. It was a perfect place to snuggle up and read books. Megan took her phone and her mug of tea over to it and sat down.
"Found your coat," her dad said. "It wasn't in your old bedroom closet. It was in the coat closet downstairs."

"Oops, sorry!"

"It's OK," Gabriel said. "I'll mail it out first thing tomorrow. I don't want you getting too cold. Have you got some warmer clothes to wear until it arrives?"

"Yeah, I've got my sweatshirt, and I think I've got some old turtlenecks I can layer under it, plus my trusty hoodie."

"How's the weather there? We're getting ten inches of snow here tonight, probably more over the next few days. Is the cold front hitting Texas also?"

"I didn't see any snow on the forecast here, Dad. It's a little cold, but I'll be fine." Megan didn't want her dad to worry about her.

"Okay, *Mija*. You stay warm though."

"I will, Dad. Love you."

"Love you too, sweetheart," Gabriel said before hanging up the phone.

Megan was right, they didn't get any snow in Austin. But they might as well have. The temperatures dropped to the 30's and 40's, not quite cold enough to freeze, but with a driving rain that sent chills into her bones. She wore all her layers to work the next morning, but she was still cold and wet when she arrived and had to peel off the top two layers and hang them in the back room to get dry again.

She was working at the counter that afternoon when Sierra and Patrice waltzed in and sat down at the bar.

"So... dish!" Sierra demanded, propping her elbows on the bar to cradle her face, and staring at Megan with a dopey grin like she was ready to gobble up the latest tabloid gossip.

"What?" Megan asked.

"Your date!" Sierra prompted. "How did it go yesterday?"

"Yah, I heard you went out with a major hottie!" Patrice added. "We need deets, pronto!"

"Exactly. When you told me about finding that cute little library, you forgot to add that there was a cute library boy to go with it!"

Megan's cheeks turned bright crimson. "Levi and I had a nice time," she said.

"Nice. Just 'nice', she says." Sierra turned to Patrice. "I think we're going to need more than that to go off of."

"Mmm, hmm," Patrice agreed, her afro bobbing up and down with her head.

Megan caved. She told them all about the amazing Xu Bing "Book from the Sky" exhibit, about going to Amy's for ice cream afterwards, and about the shared love of books that she and Levi had.

"He even said he would try reading the book I recommended to him."

"What book?"

"*Pride and Prejudice and Zombies*," Megan answered.

Patrice made a face. "Eww, that one?"

Sierra shrugged. "The movie was funny. Matt Smith played the parson in it."

"Ooh, I like him!" Patrice crooned. "He was so hot in 'The Crown.'"

"Maybe we'll make a movie-night of it sometime," Megan jumped in. "Anyways, this will be the first time Levi has read anything of Jane Austen's-- even if it is a hybrid of her work and another author's additions-- so I really hope he likes it."
Sierra smiled. "*Chica*, I saw the way he looked at you in the Blanton. Even if he thought it was the stupidest book in the whole world, he would probably tell you he liked it."
"Will you see him again?" Patrice asked eagerly.
"I have no idea. Although, I guess I do have to return the book I borrowed back to the library sometime."
"Do you have his number?" Sierra wanted to know.
Megan nodded.
"Call him!" her friend urged.
"I'm on duty right now!" she complained.
"Then send him a text. That's allowed, right?" Patrice put in.
Megan glanced around the coffee shop. It was nearly noon, and the morning rush had died down. Her friends were the only customers in the store. "OK," she agreed.
Hey, this is Megan, she began typing, but Sierra swiped the phone from her. "I'll do it," she insisted.
"Wait! No!" Megan's protests fell on deaf ears. Sierra's fingers pitter-pattered away, furiously composing a message. Before Megan could even stop her, she had sent it.
Her friend handed the phone back to Megan, a proud look on her face. Groaning, Megan looked to see what she had written.

Hey, this is Megan. If you're free today, why don't we hang out? I get off work at 3. Hope 2 C U soon! The message ended with a cute, animated emoji that was winking and blowing a kiss.

"Ugh, you had to put that emoji on there?" Megan whined. Sierra just shrugged.
"Why today?" Megan asked. "I thought girls were supposed to 'play it coy'. Make the guy wait a few days to increase suspense. Wait for him to make the next move, that sort of thing."
"That's so last-decade. Nowadays, if a girl likes a guy, she should just go after him," Sierra asserted. "Why? You got something else going on after work?"
"I just don't want to seem desperate..." Megan grimaced.
A minute later, Levi's reply came through with a "ding".
"That was fast!" Patrice exclaimed.
"Read it for us!" Sierra insisted.
Megan obliged.

Hey! Good to hear from you again. Sure, I get off at 4 today. Do you want to grab a cup of coffee someplace?

"Text him the address here!" Sierra begged.
Megan shook her head. "Absolutely not! No way am I having my next date with him at the place where I work!" Keeping the phone close so her friends couldn't snatch it, she typed her reply.

There's a coffee shop on Lamar next to Central Market. How about there? She texted him the name and address of the place.

Levi's response came almost immediately. *Sounds good. I'll meet you there. Can't wait to see you again!*

Her friends peered over her shoulder to see what he had written.
"Eee! He can't wait to see you! That's so romantic," Patrice swooned.
"Gurl," Sierra drawled. "I hope you know how lucky you are to find a guy like this."
"Stop it!" Megan blushed. "Besides, this is only our first 'real' date. That last one doesn't count because you set us up on the fly."
"And you'll have me to thank for it when you're living happily together in your little 3-bedroom house, swinging on the front porch swing with your two totally adorable chubby babies resting on your knees," Sierra daydreamed.
"Wow, you've got this all planned out, huh?" Megan said dryly.

The door to the coffee shop swung open. Megan stood up straighter, expecting a customer. But it was only Keenan, the owner's nephew, with his tartly dressed girlfriend in tow. He swaggered over to the counter. Megan wondered if he walked that way to try to look cool, or to keep his pants, which hung off his hips and exposed his plaid underwear, from completely falling down.
"Hey, can you get mocha lattes for me 'n my girl?" he asked, while Veronica plopped down at a table nearby and whipped out her phone.
"Okay, but you'll have to pay for them. Your uncle said, 'no more free drinks for you'."
Keenan groaned, but pulled his wallet from the side pocket of his sagging cargo pants. "After all I do for him, you'd think the least he could do would be to give me drinks on the house."
Megan made the drinks and handed them to Keenan.
"By the way," he said, "I'm still not feeling so hot after that bout of the flu. Would you mind takin' my shift this afternoon?"
"Sorry, Keenan, she's got a date," Sierra answered for her.
"You've got a date?" he sneered. At their table, Veronica tried to hide her chuckle behind her phone.
Patrice put her hands on her hips. "Yeah. She does. She can't take your shift. Besides, you look just fine to me."
Keenan faked a cough. "Well, I s'pose I can work, if it's all the same to you. Just

hope I don't get anybody sick or nothin'."
"I sure hope you don't get your girlfriend sick," Sierra countered. "I saw you two through the window, playing tonsil hockey on the sidewalk, before you waltzed in."

Duke entered through the back door. "Afternoon, Megan," he greeted.
"Good afternoon, Boss!" Megan replied, smiling as the pudgy man took his place beside Megan.
"Lookin' good, Duke!" Sierra waved.
"Thanks, Sierra! Though not as good as my namesake over there," Duke pointed at the photograph of Duke Ellington on the wall, whom his mom had named him after.
"Naw, you look better!" Sierra laughed.
The old man winked. "If you're trying to butter me up so you can get some free coffees, it's working."
Sierra pointed her fingers like a pair of guns and clicked her mouth. "That's my angle!"
Duke chuckled. Spotting his nephew sitting in the corner he addressed him. "Keenan, good to see you're better. I trust you'll be serving the customers on your shift this afternoon, then."
Keenan just glowered.
Turning back to Megan, Duke said, "Thanks for pulling double-duty while this fella here was out."
"Anytime, Boss."
"To reward you, I'm letting you off early for the day. I'll still pay you for the full shift, though."
"Wow, thanks!" Megan exclaimed.
"What? That's not fair!" Keenan stood up to protest.
"Keenan, you've been taking a lot of extra time off lately. Why don't you help me finish off Megan's shift then stay for your own shift?"
"No way! I'm outta here. C'mon." He motioned to Veronica, who hastily grabbed their drinks and pranced after him as fast as her tight miniskirt and 4-inch heels would allow.
"Be back at two to start work!" Duke called as the door swung.
"Whatever," Keenan said without looking back just before the door shut.

Megan was worried. "What if Keenan doesn't come back for his shift?"
"Don't fret yourself about it. I'll be here all afternoon. If he doesn't show, I'll cover for him. But he won't get paid if he does that. Veronica keeps bleeding him dry, and sooner or later, that credit card debt of his is going to catch up to him."
"Geez," Sierra remarked.
Duke turned to Megan's friends. "Now, how about those free drinks we were talking about?"

"That'd be swell, Duke, thanks!" Sierra replied. "We'll take them to go. We've got to get Ms. Vasquez here ready for her date!"
To Megan's embarrassment, they filled her boss in on the latest development in her love life while he prepped their coffees.
"Good luck on your date!" his deep voice resounded, as the three ladies headed out the door.

Sierra and Patrice took Megan back to her apartment, where they forced her to take a shower while they dug through her closet and laid out several outfits on the bed.
Megan came out of the shower wearing her bathrobe.
"This would look great on you," Sierra pointed to a cute skirt and blouse that Megan hardly ever wore.
Megan shook her head. "Too cold. Haven't you been outside? It's like, 40 degrees!"
"Yeah, but you'll be inside."
But Megan wasn't about to be swayed.
Patrice took a stab with a different outfit. "Ok, what about these leggings and this cute sweater?"
"Hmm," Megan thought. "Better. But I think I should pair it with these jeans." She swapped the sweater over to her best pair of jeans lying on the other side. A nod of affirmation. "And put a turtleneck underneath," she added.
"You'd think this girl was a nun or something," Patrice rolled her chocolate eyes at Sierra, who nodded sympathetically.
"If you're going to wear jeans, maybe you should try this sexy v-neck," Sierra made another suggestion. She pointed to a black polyester shirt with geometric patterns and three-quarter length sleeves.
"That's too dressy for a coffee date," Megan disagreed.
"Yeah, but the chunky sweater with jeans...it just screams..." Sierra hunted for the right words.
"Nineties," Patrice filled in. "That outfit looks so 1995 to me."
"Could I pair it with the skinny jeans?" Megan asked.
Patrice shrugged. "Better."
Sierra shook her head. "Girl, you want to make a good impression on this man, don't you?"
"Why? He's already seen me."
"Yeah, but this is, like, a *date*-date. It's expected that you'll put in a little more effort to look nice. This isn't just a trip to your neighborhood library."
Megan caved in. "Okay, I hear you," she said, grabbing the shirt from Sierra's hands.

When Sierra and Patrice dropped her off at the coffee shop at four-thirty, Megan was dressed in the black v-neck with her nicest pair of jeans, though she had added a camisole underneath the shirt for warmth and modesty. Her friends had convinced her to leave behind her favorite hoodie in exchange for a chic khaki blazer that she usually kept for interviews. Black boots and Sierra's gold dangle earrings, borrowed for the night, completed her ensemble. Levi was already waiting.

"Wow, you look great!" he complimented.

"Thanks," Megan blushed. "You look good too."

Levi was dressed in the same type of black jeans he'd had on the last two meetings, but instead of a long-sleeve t-shirt, he had on a button-up white shirt with a lightweight gray sweater on top of it. His black puffy coat hung over the back of his chair.

They got their drinks and sat back down at the table.

"So," Levi began, "how was work today?"

"Oh, um, it was good," Megan nodded nonchalantly.

"Since you said you work at a coffee shop, I thought maybe you would ask me to meet you there."

"I didn't want to be seen by any of the regulars or have my boss or his annoying nephew spying on us the whole time. Nobody knows me in this place," she explained.

Levi laughed. "I hear ya. I would be nervous too if our date were happening in the place where I worked."

"I'm sure Loretta would watch you like she was watching the latest telenovela on TV," Megan joked.

"That she would! She's a dear, though."

Megan agreed. "She seems very nice."

"Won't find a sweeter lady this side of the Red River. They're all nice people, the library staff. I'll have to introduce you to the rest of them next time."

Levi changed the subject. "I started reading *Pride and Prejudice and Zombies* last night."

"Yeah? What do you think?"

"So far, I like it! Just enough blood and gore to keep me entertained. But I have a question though. Why are the Bennet girls going to lose their home when their father dies?"

The prompt was enough for Megan to launch a discussion about estate entails, and why the Bennet's family home would go to their distant cousin once the patriarch died. Levi found it all fascinating. He asked many more questions about the book, all of which Megan was happy to answer for him.

"You're so knowledgeable about *Pride and Prejudice*!" Levi complimented.

Megan's ears turned pink. "Well, it is my favorite book, which I've read many times," she explained. "Plus, it helps that I just finished re-reading it. Which reminds me, I need to stop by the library later to return it."

"No problem," Levi nodded. "So, what will you read next?" he asked.

"I'm not really sure," Megan answered.

"What are you in the mood for?"

"I have no idea. I could always reread one of the classics, I guess. I never tire of them."

"Why not try something new?" Levi suggested.

"What would you recommend?"

"There's this great indie-author that I love, Taylor Hohulin. His latest book, *The Cloud*, just came out not too long ago. It's the third book in his series called *The Marian* trilogy, about this guy that gets transported to an alternate world, where all the oceans are dried up and water is a hot commodity. He ends up on this steam-powered pirate ship that goes around stealing water from the wells, and helping the crew fight the tyrants that want to control the world's water supply."

Megan was a little skeptical about whether she would like this type of book, but she didn't want to seem rude, so she said, "It sounds interesting, but kinda...bizarre too."

Levi's head bobbed up and down. "That's exactly the point. This author loves to write stuff that's a little bit weird, but his writing is so super good! I think you might like these books. They're adventure stories!"

Megan shrugged. "I guess I could give them a try. Shall we look for the first title when we go by the library later?"

Levi shook his head. "You won't find these books at our library, unfortunately. But you can get the e-book version and read it on your phone or tablet."

"I've never been one for e-books, really," Megan admitted. "I think I prefer the smell and feel of actual pages in my hands."

"I hear ya," Levi agreed. "Are you finished?" he pointed to her coffee cup on the table.

Megan nodded. "Yeah."

"Wanna head out?"

"Where are we going?"

"My place," Levi answered. "I wanna pick up something there."

This time, Megan got into Levi's car without any hesitation. They drove several minutes to a nice apartment complex. Not gated, or anything, but definitely fancier than the dump Megan lived in. Levi put the car in park outside of Building Four.

"You can come up with me if you want to. I'll only be a few minutes."

Megan's heart raced at the thought of going up to this apartment, the home of a man she barely knew. For a moment, she almost decided to just wait in the car. Then, on impulse, she threw open the car door and hurried to join Levi on the stairs.

Levi's apartment was sparsely furnished with a faux-leather couch that was peeling in a few places, a TV, an old, upholstered recliner, and a bookcase. On one side of the room, there was a small table and chairs, and two barstools by the kitchen counter. There was a closed door on another wall, which Megan presumed led to his bedroom. The apartment was neither a total pigpen, nor a pristine enclave. Stacks of mail and other papers littered the kitchen counter, negating the ability to eat or put groceries there. An empty soda can, and a paper plate had been left on the coffee table, near which a pair of socks lay forgotten on the carpet. On one corner of the couch sat a laundry basket full of clean clothes needing to be folded and put away.

"Uh, sorry about the mess," Levi apologized, hurriedly throwing away his trash from the coffee table.

"It's fine," Megan said.

"Lemme get what I came for." Levi walked to his bookshelf and pulled three titles off it. He walked back to where Megan stood near the front door and handed them to her.

She read the titles out loud. "*The Marian, The Hunted,* and *The Cloud.*" She looked up. "These are the books you were talking about!"

"Yep. I met the author, Taylor, at a steampunk convention that I went to a couple of months ago where he was promoting the third book in the set. I'd already read the first two as e-books, but I knew I had to get all three on paperback for my collection."

Megan flipped open the front cover of *The Marian*, and gasped. "It's signed by the author!"

"They all are," Levi said. "I want you to borrow these."

Megan shook her head. "I can't take your books. What if something happens to them?"

Levi shrugged. "Then they won't be in mint-condition. No big deal. *The Cloud* already has a few creases in it since that's the one I hadn't read yet at the time. It's more important that you get a chance to read these."

Megan clasped the books to her chest. "Thank you, Levi!"

Levi handed her one of the cheap reusable bags he kept for groceries. "Here, you can carry the books in this. Don't worry about returning the bag. I've got tons."

They headed back to Levi's car. "I'm hungry," Levi said. "Wanna grab some food somewhere?"

"We just had coffee," Megan reminded him.

"Yeah, but that's not food. How about some dessert at Upper Crust Bakery? It's just down the street from the library, and they serve up a mean Chocolate Italian Cream cake."

Megan remembered her slim dining-out budget and in her head rang up the price of the coffee she just had and the ice cream from the night before. "I, uh, I kinda already spent my dining-out money for the week," she admitted.

"That's OK, it's my treat. Please. You gotta try their cakes!" Levi insisted.

Megan agreed, and it wasn't long before they were both digging into the lush, chocolatey, cream-cheese frosting and moist cake at the little bakery on Burnet Road.

"You were right, Levi, this cake is amazing!" Megan exclaimed.

"Mmm, I told you!" He leaned over towards Megan. "You got a little somethin' there, I think." He motioned to his own face to direct where she should wipe. Megan tried to get the offending smear off her face with her napkin, but she kept on missing it.

"Nope, it's still there," Levi said. "Here, let me help you." Taking the napkin from her, he wiped the chocolate frosting off her skin.

Megan felt her cheeks turn pink again. "Thanks," she said.

Just then, a stylish couple walked in the bakery. Megan was seated with a view of the door, and all the pink drained from her face the second she saw who the couple was. "Oh no!" She tried to hide her face with the napkin.

Levi whipped around to see who had entered but, of course, he didn't recognize them. He turned back to Megan with a puzzled look.

"It's my ex-boyfriend, and my former boss!" Megan whispered, panic riddled all over her face.

Chapter 4

When Megan saw Brad and Kimberly walk into Upper Crust Bakery, not twenty feet away from her, she wished she could just sink into the floor and disappear. It didn't help that Kimberly looked like a perfect Barbie doll, wearing gray plaid pants and a ribbed black turtleneck that emphasized her trim figure, her platinum-bleached hair tied up in a high ponytail that showed off her flawless creamy skin. Brad looked handsome and sharp as ever in his crisp navy sport coat, with the collar of his white button-up undone just at the top button, his short brown hair perfectly spiked with gel, and his beard closely cropped. They both looked like they had just gotten off work from their office downtown. At the same startup company that Megan was supposed to be working for. If not for them.

Anger mixed with fear of being recognized swirled around inside Megan's heart. Just then, Brad and Kimberly caught a glimpse of her. Kimberly took a step back, while Brad looked around awkwardly.
Pretending to just notice her, Brad opened, "oh, uh, hi Megan. Haven't seen you in here before. We don't come here that often. Uh, we can go, if you like." Beside him, Kimberly had a pasted-on smile, but the discomfort in her eyes was clearly visible."
"No, that's OK," Megan stood up in a hurry. "We were just leaving." She grabbed her purse and made for the door, almost leaving Levi behind in her haste to escape.
"Uh, bye!" Levi called awkwardly to the two strangers to him, not wanting to be totally rude to them.

Megan rushed to Levi's car parked around the back, practically in tears by the time they got there. She pulled at the door handle a couple of times as if willing to unlock it faster, until Levi clicked his keys to open it for her. Megan tried desperately to compose herself as Levi entered the car beside her.
"I'm sorry you had to see them," he said. "Clearly, you guys didn't part on a good note."
"You could say that again," Megan scoffed. "Levi, I hate to ask you this, but do you think you could give me a lift home?"
"Sure. Of course." He started the engine while she gave him her address.

"Oh, shoot!" Megan exclaimed when they got to her apartment.
"What?"
"I forgot about returning the library book. Would you mind taking it for me?"

She held out the copy of *Pride and Prejudice* that had been in her purse.
"I don't mind. Actually," Levi said, on second thought, "why don't you keep it for now? It's got a couple more weeks left until it's due. That way, I can be sure I'll see you again."
Megan smiled. "OK. " She shoved it back inside her canvas hobo-style bag.
"Thanks for understanding about my quick exit from the bakery," she said.
"You seemed pretty upset back there. Just want you to know, if you want somebody to talk to, I'm happy to listen."
Megan considered inviting him up to her apartment, but that just seemed like a bad idea. Instead she said, "why don't we take a stroll around the neighborhood for a while? I kind of don't feel like being alone again just yet."
"Yeah, sounds good."
"Lemme just drop off these books upstairs and I'll join you."

A few minutes later, they were strolling the pathway around the large park across from Megan's apartment. The driving rain from that morning had let up, and the skies were clear, but cold.
"Brad's the reason that I moved out here to Austin," Megan said over the crunch of their feet on the gravel path.
"I thought you came out here for your job," Levi remarked.
"I did. That is, I followed Brad here to work for the same company as him. We met when I was working for the tech company in Santa Fe. He and Kimberly both worked in the same department, but they always swore they were 'just friends'. Ha, I should have known better even back then," Megan said dryly. She continued, "Not long after we met, Kimberly moved to Austin to launch her own company, and Brad and I started dating. Everything seemed so great. We were in love. Or so I thought."
"What happened?" Levi asked.
"About 6 months into the relationship, Brad got a call from Kimberly asking him to come work for her. He said it was a really great opportunity for him; would really help build his career. But I didn't know how it would work out, being in a long-distance relationship. He told Kimberly that his condition for taking the job would be that I got hired too, and she agreed. I quit my job, spent all my savings, and came out here to start the job. In the meantime, my dad, who is Catholic, said that I couldn't go live with my boyfriend unless we were engaged, at the very least. I pressured Brad into asking me to marry him, and we got a huge fancy apartment together downtown. It was way more expensive than what I thought we could afford, but Brad insisted that our sign-on bonuses would be enough to get us started, and that if the company did well, we would be getting a raise by Christmas. I thought this would be a great move for me, especially since my best friend from high school, Sierra, was already here getting her master's at UT."

They passed by a statue of a little girl chasing a butterfly.

"But I was wrong," Megan resumed her story. "Things didn't go great. I had only been here a month or so; had only been working for my new company a few weeks, when I found a bunch of texts from Kimberly on Brad's phone."
"Lemme guess," Levi interjected, "they weren't the kind of texts about work."
Megan's dry laughter rang out. "No, they were not. Turns out he had been cheating on me with Kimberly right from the start. I broke up with him, and Sierra was nice enough to let me crash with her and her roommate Patrice for a while. But I lost my whole half of the deposit on the apartment, all the money I had spent moving my stuff out there, everything. Brad wouldn't pay me back a dime, even after Kimberly moved in with him."
"Ouch!"
"Yeah. To make matters worse, she called me into the office about a day after I found out about the two of them. She said that they had recently lost some of their investors, and unfortunately, there wouldn't be enough capital for them to keep me on. Last one in, first one out, ya know," she snorted. Levi nodded in understanding. Megan continued, "I was pretty sure it was just an easy way to get rid of me, though. Not that I really wanted to stay, considering how awkward it would be seeing the two of them there every day, but I really needed the money. It would have been nice if they could have let me work from home until I found another job, at least."
"Megan, I'm so sorry all this happened to you," Levi sympathized.
Tears welled up in Megan's eyes. "Yeah, me too. At least I got my furniture back. I had to use the money my dad sent for my birthday to rent a truck and beg Brad to let me go over one Saturday to move the rest of my things over to my new apartment. He watched me the whole time, to make sure I didn't take anything that wasn't mine."
"Sheesh! What a jerk!" Levi commented. He stopped walking and took Megan's hands in his. "You deserve somebody so much better than Brad," he told her.
Megan started sobbing. "That's the thing, I'm not sure I really do. I sort of feel like I was just the stand-in for Kimberly while she was away from Brad. She's so much prettier and better dressed than I am. She and Brad look like they belong together."
"If they belong together, it's because they're both selfish dirtbags and they deserve each other," Levi stated. "But you, you're smart, and kind, and beautiful--"
"--You think I'm beautiful?" Megan was getting even more choked up now.
"--Gorgeous!"
A smile broke through Megan's tears. "Even Brad never called me that. 'Cute', 'hot' once or twice, but never 'beautiful'. Only my dad has ever called me that."
"Well, you should hear it more often. You're beautiful, Megan Vasquez." Levi inched closer. "May I kiss you?" he asked.
Megan nodded that he could.
Still holding Megan's hands, Levi closed the gap between them until mere centimeters separated their bodies. He tenderly caressed her face. Megan

instinctively closed her eyes and let her mouth part just slightly as Levi's met hers. His lips were warm and soft like velvet and smelled like the chocolate cake they had just eaten. His kiss was gentle and sweet; it made Megan feel safe and cherished. Nothing like the kisses she'd had from Brad. His were always forceful, always invading, as if they served only to give him pleasure and a sense of domination.
Levi's kiss was short. It left Megan wanting more, but not daring to ask for it. The wounds she still carried made her heart unwilling to risk more than the brief encounter they'd shared.

"Shall we walk back?" Levi asked, noticing that the sun was setting by now. Megan agreed, and the pair made a one-eighty back towards Megan's apartment. They walked quicker now, but not quick enough to spare Megan, who was growing colder by the minute as the temperatures dropped. She let out an unconscious shiver.
"Are you cold?" Levi asked. He noticed that though the weather was below forty, she only had on a thin jacket over her shirt.
"I'm OK," Megan lied. They continued on some paces, but Megan was unable to stop herself from shivering more. Her teeth began to chatter, even though she pulled the jacket closer and rubbed her hands to try to keep warm.
"You're freezing!" Levi exclaimed as he grasped her hands again to rub them together in his. "Here, you need this." He whipped off his own coat and put it around Megan's shoulders.
"But then you'll get cold!" Megan protested.
Levi shook his head. "I've got a sweater over my button-up and an undershirt beneath that. I'll be fine, trust me."
Megan was cold enough that she quit arguing and accepted his offer. She put her arms inside the coat and zipped it up. The coat was warm; layers of quilted fabric & stuffing, and a fur lining inside the hood.
"Thank you," Megan said as she pulled the hood over her head and finally stopped shivering.
"Anytime," Levi replied.
"Is Texas always this cold in December?"
"Not always. It could easily be 75 out this time of year. Or we could get a freeze. Texas weather can't seem to make up its mind in the wintertime. One day cold, the next day hot."
"How do you plan what to wear on any given day?"
"Check the weather," Levi answered. "I like to say that Texas really only has two seasons: Summer, and Not Summer."
Megan chortled. "That's great! Reminds me of a saying we had in Albuquerque: you can go skiing in the mountains in the morning and play golf in the afternoon. The weather there was notoriously unpredictable also, and often changed even in the middle of the day. Santa Fe is a bit colder though. My dad said right now they've got ten inches of snow, and this is only the beginning of

December."
"Wow! That's one thing you won't see much of here in Austin. Every few years or so, we might get some snow, but never more than a couple inches. We get ice more commonly. When that happens, the whole town seems to shut down."
"Why?" Megan asked, puzzled.
"Nobody knows how to drive on ice here," Levi explained.
His comment made Megan laugh again. They walked until they reached Megan's apartment again.

"Thanks for the walk," Megan said, "and thanks again for letting me use your coat." She began undoing the zipper and taking it off. "Hopefully, my coat will get here soon," she remarked.
"You mean you don't have a coat right now?" Levi asked as she handed his coat to him.
"My dad's sending it to me in the mail. Should be here in a couple of days. Until then, I've got my sweatshirts and hoodie to keep me warm."
"Here, take this, until your package arrives," Levi gave the coat to her again. "I've got another coat I can wear. You need this more than I do."
"Are you sure?"
Levi nodded. "One-hundred percent. I would feel terrible if I saw on the news that you froze to death on the sidewalk without a coat when I had two coats and could have spared one. I can just see the headline: Girl found dead of frostbite on 45th Street, no coat in sight."
Megan laughed once again. "Well, thank you then."
"I can't pretend to be all-altruistic. You know this is another of my tricks to ensure that I get to see you again! You bring back that coat, or else I can't be responsible for whatever crazy act I commit in order to meet you!"
"Stop it!" her laughter had her nearly doubled over in stitches.
"Seems like you're feeling better again," Levi remarked.
Megan wiped the tears of laughter from her eyes. "Yeah, I am."
"Good. Take care and have a good night." Levi gave her a quick squeeze before getting in his car. Megan wished that he had kissed her again.

Chapter 5

Over a week went by before Megan saw Levi again. Duke gave Keenan an ultimatum, come to work every day he's scheduled, or get fired. Surprisingly, Keenan started showing up when he was told to. Good news for Duke and the Enchanted Moon, but bad news for Megan, who was still short on funds. To make up for the loss of the double-shifts, Megan got a second job as a holiday salesclerk at Hobby Lobby. She knew the job would end once Christmas was over, but she hoped by then she might have gotten a better job that could replace both the coffee shop and the craft store.

Thanks to the demanding schedules of her two jobs, she had no time to go on any dates. But that didn't stop Megan and Levi from texting or calling. They talked every day, growing more and more friendly with each other all the time. When she wasn't on her phone with Levi or working, Megan read the books that he had given her. She liked *The Marian* so much that she accidentally stayed up until 2am reading it the first night and paid the price for it when she had to wake for the early morning shift at Enchanted Moon. After that, she made sure to pace herself. Nevertheless, she finished all three books before she saw Levi again.

It was her day off at Enchanted Moon, and she didn't have to be at her other job 'til afternoon, so Megan walked to the library to return *Pride and Prejudice*. She knew Levi was working that morning, so she decided to surprise him. Loretta smiled and said "hi" as she walked in. As she dropped the book off with Loretta, she saw Levi shelving books in the non-fiction section. Setting his coat and her purse on a nearby chair, she snuck up behind him and put her hands over his eyes. "Guess who?" she teased.
"The President of the United States," Levi joked. He took her hands from his face and spun to look at her.
"I'm surprised to see you here today."
"Why? Were you expecting someone else?"
Levi smiled and shook his head. "Not at all."
"I brought you your coat back," she said, handing him the coat and putting her purse back on her shoulder.
"And I see that you've got yours now too," he apprised the puffy blue coat she wore. It was almost the same as Levi's, except for the color.
"Looks like we're going to be twinsies in these!" he laughed.
Megan chuckled along with him.

Levi glanced around at the empty library. "Hey Loretta," he called, "I'm gonna take my break now, OK?"
Loretta's dark eyes twinkled at the couple. "Sure thing, honey. Take an extra-long break if you like."
"Thanks!"

Levi and Megan settled comfortably into the corner armchairs.
"So, I uh, finished the books you lent me," Megan said, pulling a grocery bag containing the three books from her oversized purse and handing it to Levi.
"Wow, that was quick!"
Megan blushed. "What can I say? I'm a fast reader."
"What did you think of them?" he asked her.
"They were amazing!"
"Aren't they? I knew you would love them!"
"So many plot twists...like how they managed to get rid of the bad guy in the end, who the mole turned out to be..."
"It's insane, right?" Levi grinned.
"Totally!" Megan agreed. "But I could hardly put them down. I had to pace myself so I wouldn't end up staying up all night reading."
Levi laughed. "Some of us would have just done that and finished them all at once."
"Yeah, well, some of us have to be up for a 6am shift at a coffee shop!"

They talked for several more minutes about the plot intricacies of *The Marian* series, who their favorite characters were, and so on.
Then Levi said, "Hey, I get off at six. Wanna go with me to see the Trail of Lights tonight?"
"I can't," Megan winced. "I have to work at Hobby Lobby this afternoon until eight."
"That's OK. It's open pretty late." He looked up the website on his phone. "It says here that they're open until ten. Want me to pick you up from your work and we can go?"
"Okay," Megan nodded. She stayed for a while and checked out some more books that Levi recommended. When it was time to head out to her afternoon job, she waved goodbye to Levi.
"I'll see you at eight!" he said, returning her wave.
Her shift at Hobby Lobby had never seemed to drag on as long as it did that day. It felt like time itself had warped and slowed down to a crawl, as she spent the hours re-shelving merchandise, cutting fabric in the sewing department, ordering custom frames in the framing department, helping customers find whichever aisle was needed for their particular hobby, and checking them out. Even with the extra help they'd hired on, there weren't enough employees to man all the stations at once, so they took turns going to each department whenever a customer there needed help, and calling more employees to the

cashier stations whenever the lines got too long. Megan was thoroughly exhausted from running all over the store by the time the little hand on the clock finally pointed to eight. She hung up her apron in the back room and washed her hands before leaving into the back parking lot. True to his word, Levi was waiting for her there with his car running.

"Hey there," he greeted as she hopped into his car. "How was work?"
"I'm so pooped," she sighed.
"I'll bet. Here, this is for you." He handed her a sub sandwich from a local shop just before he started driving.
"It's turkey on whole wheat. I hope that's OK."
"It's great! Thank you, you didn't have to get me anything," Megan beamed.
"There's drinks too. I didn't know what you like, so I got one Coke and one unsweet tea. I haven't drank either of them. You pick first."
"I'll take the tea. Tea's my favorite. Thanks again."
"I'm glad you picked the tea. I much prefer soda, anyways," Levi admitted.
Megan laughed. "Well, I'm glad you got unsweet instead of sweet tea. I can't stand that stuff."
"Really? That's the only way I can drink it. But I didn't know if you would, so I got unsweet and grabbed some packets of sugar from the beverage station, just in case."
"You really thought of everything, didn't you?"
"I tried," Levi grinned. "My motto is the same as the Boy-Scout's: 'be prepared'," he laughed.
Just then, Levi's car went over a pothole in the road, causing Megan to drip mustard from her sandwich onto her jeans. "Oh no!" she exclaimed. "Do you have any napkins?"
Levi smacked his forehead. "I knew there was something I forgot! So much for being 'Mr. Boy-scout'. Uh...check the glove compartment. Maybe there's some in there."
Megan shuffled around in the compartment until she found some wrinkled napkins from a burger joint. As she pulled out the stack, a photograph fell onto the floor.
"Who's this?" Megan asked as she picked up the picture of Levi with his arm around a pretty brunette.
Levi glanced at the photo as they came to a red light. "Oh, that's my ex-girlfriend. I must have forgotten that it was in there. I don't open the glove box that often. You can throw that away," he motioned to the trash bag hanging from his dashboard.
Megan took a final glance at the woman in the photo before stuffing the picture in between old Styrofoam cups and wrappers in the trash bag. For some reason, the woman looked vaguely familiar to her. But maybe she just had that sort of ubiquitous look, Megan thought.

They drove for a few minutes before Megan spoke again. "So, how long ago since you broke up?"

"Wha--? Oh, uh, I guess it was about August, I think." Levi shrugged. "She was kinda crazy, as it turned out."

"Were you two together long?"

"About a year. We met in one of our classes together. But things were never all that great between us. She was always threatening to break up over stupid stuff, then the next day she'd wanna get back together. I finally got tired of all her drama and told her it was quits for good. She was leaving town anyway, so it was good timing."

Megan was about to ask the ex-girlfriend's name, but just then, a giant Christmas tree made of lights came into view.

"Woah, what's that?" Megan gasped.

"That's the big tree at the end of the Trail of Lights," Levi explained.

"It's amazing!"

"Sure is. Just wait until you're standing underneath it."

Megan's jaw dropped. "We can do that?"

"You bet!"

They exited the freeway and turned left underneath the overpass towards Zilker Park. Levi flashed the parking pass he'd downloaded on his phone, and the guard let them into a parking lot at the entrance to the park.

"The trail starts over this way," Levi gestured in the direction the crowds of people were walking from the parking lot towards the glowing lights of the holiday display.

Megan was spellbound. The lights had seemed pretty enough at a distance, but as they grew close, the whole thing seemed magical. A huge glowing archway spelled out the words "Trail of Lights". As they walked through it, they were surrounded by thousands of tiny Christmas lights lining the sides of the man-made "tunnel". Ahead of them, a wonderland of twinkling, glowing lights wound around the park. Hundreds of trees were covered from tips-to-trunk in bright colored strands. Beneath them, decorative displays of cute characters or giant candies stood out in the spotlights. There was a life-size gingerbread house, a Cinderella's coach, a bandstand where local musicians and dancers performed, a carousel, and even a Ferris wheel!

"This is so incredible!" Megan exclaimed. "Sierra talked about this event after she went last year, but I had no idea just how cool it was. She wasn't overreacting when she said this place is over the moon!"

"I'm glad you like it," Levi said. "What should we do first? The carousel? The Ferris wheel?"

"Let's go over and hear that band," she pointed at the stage where an indie rock group was just starting up their set. They turned out to be really good. Megan was impressed.

"They don't call this, the 'live music capital of the world' for nothing," Levi remarked when he heard her praise for them. "A lot of great musicians get their start here. Did you make it out here for the Austin City Limits music fest this year?"

Megan shook her head. "No, I was too busy wallowing in self-pity at the time. I heard about it from Sierra though. She likes to go to all the big festivals in town."

After the rock group finished their performance, a polka band came on stage, prompting Levi, who wasn't a big fan of polka, to suggest that they move on. "Wanna hit the carousel next?"

Megan nodded. They bought tickets for the big, old-fashioned carousel. When their turn came to board, Megan chose a beautiful white horse. Beside her, Levi hopped onto a stunning black stallion.

"Wanna race?" he joked.

"I dunno," Megan laughed. "I think we might come out a tie either way."

"Unless I can make these horses jump off the carousel, like Mary Poppins did," Levi quipped.

"Have you got some magic nanny-powers that I don't know about?" Megan asked, the grin on her face getting wider by the minute.

"Who knows?" Levi wiggled his eyebrows up and down, making Megan laugh so hard she nearly fell off her horse.

"Careful there!" he cautioned.

The carousel started moving, whirling them around and around as the calliope music played. The park around them seemed to blur into a psychedelic vortex of lights and colors. Megan looked over at Levi. His face seemed to be stuck in a smile. She realized that she hadn't stopped smiling either since they got on. For a few brief minutes, when all they could see were the lights of the carousel and each other, it felt like they were in their own little world, moving up and down in a magical dance together. No one else seemed to exist on that plane; just the two of them. Then, like a spell being broken, the carousel slowed to a stop and the world around them returned to normal.

Megan was still slightly dizzy when they stepped off the carousel. Tripping over a stray tree root unseen on the ground, she began to stumble, but Levi caught her arm to prevent her from falling.

"Steady there!" he cautioned, pulling her close to him. Their sudden nearness made Megan's heart tremble with excitement. She looked up at him and smiled. On impulse, Levi planted a kiss on Megan's cheek, sending all the butterflies in her stomach into sudden flight within her. For the moment, she felt safe, happy. All thoughts of Brad and Kimberly were gone from her mind.

They walked by Cinderella's coach next, and Levi insisted they take a picture. Megan posed for him, holding out her imaginary skirt and curtsying.

"You make a perfect princess," he complimented. "Are you sure your name's

not Meghan Markle?" he teased, sending Megan into a fit of giggles. Levi sure knew how to make her feel like a giddy schoolgirl.
A passerby saw them and offered to take a picture, which they readily accepted. Levi got down on one knee and had Megan put her foot on top of his leg, while he pretended to be trying a glass slipper onto her foot.
"You guys are adorable," the lady said as she snapped the picture.
"Thanks!" Levi chirped as he grabbed a side hug with Megan for a second picture.
As they continued on the path, Levi showed the pictures off. "These turned out great!" Megan agreed. Levi tapped a few buttons. "There, I sent these to you."
"Awesome, now I can always remember our magical date," she bobbed her head.
"Wanna go do the Ferris wheel next?" Levi asked, grabbing Megan's hand, and dragging her towards it.
Suddenly, the butterfly feeling in her stomach turned from a light flutter to a grip of panic. Megan tried to protest that she would rather not do the Ferris wheel, but somehow, she couldn't get the words to come out of her mouth. Words echoed in her mind, *stop being such a baby, Megan!* She pursed her lips together. *I won't succumb to fear this time,* she thought. As they stood in line, Levi was so excited, he failed to notice how pale and trembling Megan looked.
"The Ferris wheel is my favorite," he said. "Ever since I went on the big one at the State Fair as a kid, I've always loved them."
Megan did not want to disappoint Levi, so when it was their turn to board the carriage, she gritted her teeth and took Levi's hand as he pulled her aboard.

This is fine. I'm fine, Megan told herself as the big wheel with its flashing lights began to revolve, lifting them into the sky. As they soared over treetops with the wind whipping Megan's hair in a crazy dance, she looked out over the sparkling trees of the Trail of Lights. *The view is pretty amazing up here,* she thought as she tried to focus on the scenery instead of her rattled nerves.
"You can see the whole trail from up here," Levi commented aloud, echoing Megan's unspoken thoughts. "It's great, huh?"
"Yeah," was all Megan could get out as she gripped the side of the car and tried to enjoy the ride. Suddenly, the ride halted to let more passengers on, while their car was perched at the very top of the Ferris wheel. An ornery grin came over Levi's face.
"Wanna have some fun?"
Megan shook her head, but Levi, being a tease, began to rock the car back and forth.
"Whee!" he shouted.
"This isn't funny!" Megan cried, squeezing her eyes tight.
"Don't worry, we're safe up here, and we've got our seat belts on," Levi shrugged, and continued rocking.
"I mean it, don't do this. STOP IT!" she shouted at the top of her lungs.

"Okay, I'm stopping," Levi complied, surprised at the severity of her reaction to his teasing. Tears were streaming down Megan's face now. Just then, the Ferris wheel lurched and began rotating again.

Megan screamed in terror.

"It's OK," Levi grabbed her hand to try to comfort her, but it was no use.

"I want to get off!" she shouted. "Stop the ride! Let me off!"

Fortunately for Megan, the ride operator heard her call. As soon as their car reached the base, he stopped the wheel again and allowed them to disembark. Megan practically bolted out of the car, running ahead of Levi and sobbing.

Chapter 6

Levi's legs were longer than Megan's and he caught up to her before she had gone too far.

"Hey, wait! I'm sorry!" He reached out to Megan and tried to hug her, but she pushed him away.

"How could you do that to me?" she demanded. "Didn't you see I was scared?"

"I didn't know you had a fear of heights!" he insisted. "How was I supposed to know you'd get so freaked out?"

"It's called 'body-language', and if you had any sense, you would have noticed that I wasn't comfortable. And if that didn't work, you could have listened the first time I yelled for you to stop doing it!" Megan was still crying, though her voice was angry. She stalked over to a nearby bench and sat down.

"I want to go home!" she wailed.

Levi was thoroughly ashamed of himself. He sat down on the bench beside her, hoping she wouldn't run off again, or worse-- push him off the bench onto the pavement.

He tried again to apologize. "I'm sorry, Megan. Really. I am," he said in a soft, tender voice. "Will you forgive me for being such an idiot?"

Through her tears, Megan nodded. Levi put his arm around her gently.

"B--B--Brad did the same thing to me o--one time," Megan stammered. "O-only he didn't stop at all when I asked him to. He just said I was a 'big baby' and kept on shaking the Ferris wheel car the rest of the ride. Th-then he teased me about it the rest of the day, and even told his friends about it, and they laughed too."

"Wow," Levi raked his hands through his hair. "I'm an even bigger jerk than I thought. I had no idea your ex-boyfriend put you through the same thing. Honestly, Megan, if I had known about your fears, about any of this, I never would have teased you up there. I promise I won't do something like that again."

Megan nodded. "I believe you."

"C'mere," Levi turned her towards him and put his other arm around her as well. For a few minutes, he just let Megan sob onto his shoulder, her tears soaking his jacket. His embrace was cathartic. As she released all her fears and stress, Megan calmed back down. Her sobs soon dwindled to sniffles, and soon they stopped altogether.

"Do you still want me to take you home?" Levi asked.

"I'm OK, now," Megan said as one last shudder left her body.

"Do you want to go see the rest of the trail?"

Megan nodded. "You did promise to show me the tree."

"That's right, I did! We can't leave without seeing the tree!"

The holiday tree was at the end of the Trail of Lights. Levi explained to her that it was one of the fourteen moonlight towers scattered throughout Austin, the only place left in the world to still have these towers, which were originally erected to provide light at nighttime to parts of the city. This tower was the only one that got decorated with lights every year in December, though.

"Neat," Megan commented. But 'neat' didn't even begin to describe the tree. The central structure supporting the lights resembled a cell phone tower, the way the metal bars interconnected to form a tall, straight, column rising into the sky. But at the top of the tower, the bright, LED-lit star-shaped lights shone in every direction, lighting up the park beneath it. Suspended from the center, long strands of brightly colored lights tiered down to the support poles that formed a wide circle around it, lending a conical shape to the structure. It had been magnificent when Megan saw it in the distance upon approach to the park. Now that she was up close to it, it was positively the most brilliant tree of lights she had ever seen up close.

"You gotta try this," Levi said as he stepped underneath the great canopy of lights. Standing as close to the center as he could, he looked upwards and began to spin around rapidly. Laughter radiated from him as he stumbled from getting dizzy.

Megan shook her head as she laughed at him. "You're crazy, you know."

"C'mon," Levi urged, taking her hands, "do it with me."

With reckless abandon, Megan copied Levi and threw her head up to the sky. Holding hands tightly, they spun together. The blinding circle of lights began to blur into a spiraling vortex that whirled around and around in seeming opposition to them. Megan was dizzy, but Levi seemed to have no intention of stopping their momentum.

"Don't let go!" Megan shrieked in delight. Finally, they were both so dizzy, they slowed down and let the lights return to their normal static appearance above their heads. Megan staggered a little.

"Now, we go the other way to undo our dizziness," Levi said, starting to spin in the opposite direction with her.

"Noooo!" Megan squealed, but this time, it was obvious she really wanted him to continue. They spun around and around, laughing the whole time, until they were finally both sick of spinning.

Near the tree, Levi spotted a "Hey Cupcake" truck. "I'm hungry," he decided aloud. "Wanna get some dessert?"

"Sure," Megan agreed. They each picked out a luscious-looking cupcake.

"You know," she said as they walked away from the stand, "today is Jane Austen's birthday."

"Oh yeah!" Levi exclaimed. "I should have remembered. I've only seen the sign for it in the library this whole month. I'd forgotten it was today, though. Hey, we've got our cakes now. We should sing 'Happy Birthday' to her." He

proceeded, in very loud, bravado fashion, to sing the song in Jane's honor, making Megan laugh all the more as he did, despite the strange looks they were getting from other people.
They sat down to eat their cupcakes.
"I usually celebrate Jane's birthday every year by making tea and scones and watching the whole six-hour *Pride and Prejudice* miniseries. You know, the one with Colin Firth in it."
"Is that what you'd be doing right now, if we weren't here?" Levi asked.
Megan shook her head. "Nope. I left my DVD collection back in Santa Fe. Didn't have enough room for it when I came out here. Truth be told, I don't even have a TV at my place."
"When's your next day off?" Levi wanted to know.
"I have a half-day on Sunday. I'm still working at the coffee shop in the morning, but the craft store is closed on Sundays, thankfully."
"How about we see if the library has a copy of the series, or rent it online? I bet it's on Hulu or Prime. If we have enough time, we can watch *Pride and Prejudice and Zombies* too. Did you know they made a movie about it?"
Megan nodded. "I watched it once when it came out in theaters earlier this year."
"We should watch it together! I finished the book the other day. It was great! Then I found out there was another one called *Sense and Sensibility and Sea Monsters,* and I started reading that one," Levi told her.

Megan was so pleased to see Levi taking an interest in Jane Austen. She made plans with him to come over to his place after she got off work on Sunday, and they would have a big movie marathon together.

But, as it turned out, their eight-hour movie marathon never happened. Sunday morning, when Megan walked into Enchanted Moon, Duke had a frown on his face.
"Keenan bailed out today. He and Veronica took off to Dallas for some comic-book convention he wanted to attend. I'd cover his shift, but I have to get back home today. My mother-in-law just had surgery, and she's staying at our house for a few days to recover. My wife is at her wits-end trying to take care of her. She needs all the help I can give her. Would you be able to help out this afternoon?"
Megan was about to apologize and say that she already had plans, but the dwindling numbers in her bank account reminded her that she could use any extra money she could get her hands on. So, she said 'yes' to Duke, then sent a text to Levi explaining and apologizing for why she had to bail on him. Luckily, he understood.

Hey, no worries, it's totally fine. If you want, I'll be happy to come by the coffee shop and hang out with you there instead. I really wanna see you again.

Megan couldn't deny that she wished to see him again too, and it would provide some consolation for missing their movie fest. She texted him the address of Enchanted Moon. She didn't expect him to get there so quickly, though. Within ten minutes, before Duke had gone, Levi showed up. Megan's face brightened the moment he walked in the door. Duke noticed immediately and watched the warm interaction between Megan and Levi before the latter sat down with his cup of coffee. Megan had to go to the back to grab some more milk from the supply fridge.
"Who's that?" Duke asked her when they were out of Levi's earshot.
Megan's ears turned pink. "Oh, that's my friend, Levi," she said.
Duke's eyes twinkled. "Your friend, huh? The one you had that date with?" The blush now spreading all over Megan's face told him it was. "Must be going well," Duke remarked. "Feel free to chat with him whenever the store's not too busy, but uh, don't neglect the other customers, and don't give him too many free drinks." Duke winked at her.
"I won't, Boss," she said.
"I know," Duke nodded with a big grin. "I gotta beat it. My wife just texted me that her mom needs me to pick up her prescription and some other stuff on the way home."
"Good luck!" Megan wished him.
"You too!" Duke returned as he headed out the back door.

It was peak morning hours, and the shop was packed. Levi pulled out *Sense and Sensibility and Sea Monsters* to occupy himself while Megan ran the counter nonstop. He smiled or winked at her from time to time, sending warm, gooey feelings through Megan's heart every time. The rush finally died down by early afternoon, and Megan had a chance to take a break. She fixed two blended coffee drinks and grabbed some muffins from the case for her and Levi before sitting down with him.
"I hope this is okay," she said. "Duke said we could treat ourselves before he left. He always lets me help myself to whatever's in the bakery case when I'm on my breaks."
"This is perfect. Blueberry's my favorite," Levi mumbled over a big bite of muffin. He chased it down with a swig of the mochaccino drink she'd brought him. "Thanks!" he said.

Megan's break didn't last long. A few minutes later, a big group of customers came in, and Megan had to get back behind the counter. The customers were all college students, a study group that often came in on Sunday afternoons together to drink coffee and work. They were all dressed in hipster style clothing. And as usual, they all ordered cappuccinos and lattes. Megan got right to work filling their orders, but something was wrong. She'd been using the espresso machine all morning with no issues, but now, when she turned the steam wand on, no steam was coming out. She tried tapping it several times, but still nothing. She turned to look at the crowd of customers, standing around waiting for their drinks, and a feeling of panic settled in.

Levi spotted the look on her face and came over. "What's wrong?" he whispered.
"The steam isn't working on the machine!" she told him in a hushed voice. Levi went behind the counter to help Megan.
"I've got to get all these drinks out, but I can't do it if the steam won't come out," Megan explained.
Levi nodded. "Maybe the wand is clogged by something."
"It was working fine a little bit ago!"
"I can check to see if there's an obstruction. But first, we've got to fill these orders. Do you have a French press around anywhere?"
"What's a French press?" Megan asked. "I've never used one."
Levi looked around the kitchen area until he found a small glass beaker caged in a metal frame with a handle. Attached to the lid inside the beaker was a metal plunger shaped like a disk with a mesh filter on it. "This is a French press," he explained. "Coffee or milk goes in the bottom, then you use the plunger to press it or mix it. Is the brew head on the espresso maker still working?"
Megan nodded. "Yes, I can make the coffee just fine, but I don't think they all just want espresso shots with no milk."
"It's fine. We can steam the milk in the microwave and use the French press to froth it. Why don't you make the coffees, and I'll do the milk?" Levi suggested.
Megan agreed, and handed him an apron to don. She brewed each cup of espresso and lined them up like an assembly line, while Levi microwaved the milk in a measuring glass with a thermometer to get to the right temperature, then poured it into the French press and pumped the plunger repeatedly until the milk was nice and foamy in texture. Then, he expertly poured the milk into the cup she had prepared, finishing the top with a fancy latte heart. He repeated the steps for each cup of coffee, working quickly so that the drinks would not get cold. Within a matter of minutes, they had filled all the orders.
"Wow, that was amazing! How did you get so good at making lattes and cappuccinos?" Megan asked.
"Well, I told you my parents own a little coffee shop in Old Town Spring, Texas. What I didn't tell you was that when I was in High School, I helped out all the time in the store. I had to learn how to make all the different kinds of coffee; had to fix their old machine a few times too."
"I'd say you turned out to be a pretty good barista!" Megan complimented.
"Thanks!" Levi smiled. "Now, let's see if we can figure out what's wrong with this machine." He unplugged the machine and waited several minutes for it to cool down completely. When it was safe, he unscrewed the steam wand from the machine.

"Maybe there's a problem with the valve," he said. Opening the top of the machine, he unscrewed the valve from the boiler. When he flipped the lever to test it, air easily blew through the valve.
"Okay, it must be the wand that's blocked," he diagnosed. He ran some hot water through the wand. "Do you have any pipe cleaners handy?" Levi asked.
"Uh, I think I saw some in a drawer in the back. I never knew what Duke used them for."
"Probably for cleaning things like this out," Levi said. Megan fetched the pipe cleaners, and Levi twisted a few of them together until he had a tool the right width to snake up the steam wand. As he pulled it out the other end, a bunch of calcium and mineral deposits could be seen on the pipe cleaner. "I think we've found the source of our problem!" he exclaimed. He repeated the cleaning process twice over with some new pipe cleaners until all the debris was gone, then ran the wand through hot water again for good measure. "Let's see if that did the trick." He screwed it back onto the machine and tried again. A fresh spout of steam poured from the wand.
"You did it!" Megan clapped. Instinctively, she threw her arms around Levi's neck and planted a kiss on his cheek. Levi returned the gesture by grabbing her waist and kissing her lips swiftly. The taste of coffee still lingered on both of their lips, exciting their senses.
One of the freshman college students happened to be near the counter grabbing some napkins and saw their exchange. "Ugh, PDA. Gross!" She wrinkled her nose as she returned to her seat.
Megan put her hand to her lips, embarrassed that they'd got caught.
The rest of the afternoon passed without incident. To her surprise, Levi continued to help her out behind the counter, which made her work all the more fun. She was still relieved when it was time to close up at six, though.

"Thank you so much for all your help, Levi," she smiled when the last customer left and she locked the door.
"Of course! Anything I can do to spend more time with you is worth it to me."
Megan's phone rang. It was Sierra.
"Do you mind if I answer this?" Megan asked.
"Go right ahead."
Megan punched the green button on her phone as she walked a short distance away. "Hey Sierra," she greeted.
"Hey *Chica*! Whatcha doin'?"
"I'm closing up at work."
"What? I thought Hobby Lobby is closed on Sundays."
"It is. I'm at Enchanted Moon. Keenan blew off work again, so Duke asked if I could help out."
"That doofus!" Sierra complained. "Duke ought to drag him by his cornrows and make his lazy butt do some work!"
"Yeah, tell me about it."

"So, now that you're off, do you wanna go for some dinner at Kerbey Lane?"
"I'm sorta hanging out with Levi right now," Megan said.
"I thought you said you're at work-- wait, is Levi with you right now?"
"Yeah," Megan smiled. "He came over to sit at the coffee shop while I worked but ended up saving my butt when the steamer on the espresso machine broke." She told Sierra all the details of what happened.
"You know you've got a keeper there, right?"
"Yeah, I think I do this time," Megan blushed, hoping that Levi couldn't overhear them.
"Okay, we'll do Kerbey next time. Maybe you can bring Levi with you!" Sierra said. "Have fun!"

They said their goodbyes and Megan returned to Levi.
"Sorry, I couldn't help overhearing you," Levi admitted, making Megan's ears turn pink. What had he heard? "You said we're still hanging out? Does that mean you still want to do something after this?"
"Well, I was hoping maybe we could still squeeze in a movie tonight. Not the whole six-hour miniseries; just the zombie version. It's only about two hours."
"Yeah, I'm good with that!" Levi answered.

They drove over to Levi's' place. It was nice having someone to drive her around, Megan thought. Though perhaps she was getting a bit spoiled.
They made some microwave popcorn and a frozen pizza, opened some soda and a big bag of M&Ms, and soon they were settled on Levi's couch with their food and drinks spread all over the coffee table. Two hours flew past. Levi really liked the movie. He got a kick out of seeing the Bennet girls whipping daggers from underneath their ball gowns to fight the zombies and declared that Lady Catherine de Bourgh was "quite the tough old broad."
"That first proposal scene really kicks butt!" he also said. Megan asked him how the movie compared to the book, and he had a spirited discussion over the differences.
"That Darcy guy is really something, huh?" Levi commented. "I can see now why all the girls swoon over him."
Megan smiled and hugged his arm. "Yeah, he's kinda the gold-standard for a lot of us Austenites."
"Hey, I'm an Austinite too! You know, an A-U-S-T-I-N-ite," Levi joked.
"Well, I'm doing my best to make you into an A-U-S-T-E-N-ite too," Megan laughed.
"That's good. Then, I can be an Austenite-Austinite!"
Megan snorted into her can of soda. "You're too funny!" she giggled.
"And you're too adorable," Levi said. Drawing close to her on the couch, he snaked his hands through her curly hair to cradle her head and brought her lips close to his. Megan closed her eyes and melted into his kiss. Opening her mouth slightly, she savored the salty taste from the popcorn on his lips mixed with the

sweetness of the M&Ms as his tongue lightly grazed hers. Megan put her hands on his firm shoulders as Levi deepened the kiss, enjoying all the tenderness she had to offer him. He let his hands wander down her back as he continued to kiss her, finally resting them on her hips. Megan's skin tingled with goosebumps of nervous excitement and pleasure. She stroked his face and neck, which turned him on even more. In a surge of passion, he laid her down on the couch, his arms sliding up towards her chest. Suddenly, Megan pushed him away, panic flooding her senses.

"Stop!" she yelled. She stood up and walked away from him, her breathing jagged from their heated make-out session.

Chapter 7

"What's the matter?" Levi asked. "Did I do something wrong?"
Megan wiped a tear from her eye before Levi could see it and turned back to him. "I'm sorry," she apologized. "I'm just not ready for this. I think we're moving too quickly."
"It's okay, don't be sorry," he said. "I'm glad you were honest with me."
Megan blinked back more tears as she stood with her arms crossed, not saying anything.
"Wanna take a walk instead?" Levi suggested. Megan nodded. Levi grabbed their coats and they headed out to circle the neighborhood.

"For the record, I wasn't planning on doing anything more than kissing," Levi felt he had to state.
Megan ducked her head in an attempt to hide the pink in her cheeks. She knew what she had thought they were headed towards.
"I know you've been hurt real bad," Levi said. "I'm willing to take things as slow as you need us to. And also, I think that sex is something that should be saved for marriage."
Megan looked up in surprise. "What makes you say that?"
Levi's voice began to get choked up. It took him a moment to compose himself while they walked. "Look," he finally began, "I won't pretend I'm perfect. My last girlfriend...let's just say I wasn't with her for her personality," he gave a wry grimace. "I did some things I'm not proud of, things that go against my upbringing."
"Your upbringing?" Megan asked.
"My dad's a preacher. Did I ever tell you that?"
Megan shook her head. "I thought your parents owned a coffee shop."
"They do. But they didn't start that until I was in High School. My dad graduated from seminary as a Baptist minister. I was known as the 'preacher's kid' my whole life. Later on, they wanted to start a ministry to help the people we support in the Dominican Republic. The villagers grow the coffee that we import and sell, and the profit from the store goes back to help the village school."
"That's so neat!" Megan said.
"Anyways," Levi continued, I always got 'the talk' from them about what *not* to do with the girls I dated. I kept it up pretty well-- at least, until I got to college. I guess being around so many other people that were all doing whatever they liked, I started thinking that it didn't matter anymore, until I began to compromise my values. I still have regrets about that."

Megan looked over and noticed that Levi was crying. Without meaning to, tears started falling down her own cheeks. "I didn't do such a great job of it either," she admitted. "I think I told you my dad's Catholic, so I pretty much got the same speeches you did my whole life. I too pledged that I would save myself for marriage. I held my ground all through High School, and even college, never did anything more than kiss my boyfriends. But Brad...well, he wanted more. Always pushed me for more. I never let him get 'all the way' with me, but I definitely did things, things that I would be ashamed if my dad found out about. But it still wasn't enough for him. I still wonder if my unwillingness to take the final step is the reason that he started cheating on me."

"Hey, hey!" Levi shook his head. "His behavior is in no way a reflection on you! He's the scumbag, regardless of what you were willing to do or not do. I'm pretty sure the outcome would have been the same, even if you'd given in to his advances."

"You're probably right, but it still hurts!" Megan sobbed.

"I know." Levi pulled Megan to him and let her cry on his shoulder. He couldn't seem to staunch the drizzle running down his own face either.

At last, like the cleansing of a summer rain, their shared tears seemed to wash away some of the pain in both of their hearts. Megan stopped crying and looked into Levi's face. Though tears still glistened in his eyes, he was smiling at her. Like a rainbow after a storm, it lit up Megan's heart from the inside out, until she found that the corners of her mouth had formed a smile too.

Releasing Megan from his embrace and taking her hand, Levi asked, "shall I drive you home?"

Megan nodded. "Yes, that would be great." They walked hand in hand back to Levi's apartment. As they got into Levi's car, Megan said, "I'm really glad we had this day together."

"Me too." Levi squeezed her hand before putting the car into gear.

A few days passed before they saw each other again. Megan was so busy with work, she barely had time to eat. Who knew a craft store and a coffee shop would be so busy during this time of year? But it was the week before Christmas, and finals were over at last for the college students, who now had more time to socialize. Megan read a text from Sierra on her break at Hobby Lobby.

Wanna grab some grub tonight?

I can't, I'm at work, Megan replied.

Chica, y tu no tienes have time for your best friend anymore, eh? ;-)

Megan chuckled. *LOL,* she typed, *I'll always have time for you, but I don't get off until 8. Is that OK?*

Sure! Sierra texted back. *Can we do Kerbey? I've been dying for their queso again.*

Yeah, we can do Kerbey. I know it's your fave. :-)

Around 8:30, Megan met Sierra at the Kerbey Lane Cafe and they got a booth together. Sierra must have been starving. She ordered their signature queso and bottomless chips, plus the featured fish tacos. Despite having worked all day, Megan didn't have too big of an appetite. She ordered her favorite, a stack of chocolate-chip pancakes, knowing Sierra would likely share the chips and queso with her too. The eclectic diner, open 24 hours, served a wide menu of breakfast staples, American and Tex-mex dishes, and unique seasonal dishes, even a good selection of vegetarian and vegan options. Something for everyone. Which was good, because just as soon as they placed their orders, Sierra got a call from Patrice and another friend of theirs, and since they were in the neighborhood, Sierra invited them to come by and join them.

Patrice and Brooklyn arrived not five minutes later and squished into the booth beside Megan and Sierra. Patrice knew exactly what she wanted: a veggie burger with home fries. Brooklyn, who was also a vegetarian, was less familiar with the menu though, and took a long time deciding. "I don't know if I should get the fried avocado tacos, or the vegan pancakes," she said. "Excuse me," she asked the waiter. "Are the vegan pancakes also gluten free?"
"Um," the waiter paused, "we have gluten free pancakes, and we have vegan pancakes, but I'm not sure we have ones that are both."
"Could you check?"
"Sure, ma'am." He went to the kitchen to ask and returned a minute later. "Yes, ma'am, the waiter said he could use the gluten-free mix to make the vegan pancakes for you."
"Oh, it's okay, I decided to go with the avocado tacos instead," she said, much to his irritation. "Yes, ma'am. Will that be all for y'all?"
"Actually, I changed my mind," Brooklyn said. "I'll have the pancakes after all, and a side of the vegan queso."
"What flavor?" he asked.
"Excuse me?"
The waiter repeated his question. "What flavor on the pancakes, ma'am?"
"Oh." Brooklyn took a look at the menu again. "I guess I'll have the lemon poppy seed ones."
"Sure thing," the waiter replied. "So lemme see, I've got the gluten-free, vegan, lemon poppy seed pancakes, a side of vegan queso, and a veggie burger with home fries. Coming right up!"
Megan tried hard not to laugh at the expression on the waiter's face as he left. It was a good thing Brooklyn was sitting on the other side of the table and couldn't

see it. Patrice and Brooklyn were more Sierra's friends than hers. She liked Patrice well enough, but Brooklyn could be a pain sometimes.

Brooklyn flipped her red hair behind her shoulders and leaned in closer to share her latest gossip. "So, you'll never guess who I talked to today."

"Who?" Sierra asked.

"Renee," Brooklyn answered.

Patrice groaned.

"What? She's still my friend," Brooklyn retorted.

"Isn't she that roommate you had, Patrice, before Sierra moved in with you?" Megan asked.

"Yes," Patrice answered.

When Sierra first arrived in Austin, she had a tiny apartment through the university. Patrice, Renee, and Brooklyn shared a suite in the dorms at the time, but Patrice did not get along well with Renee. She was an even bigger drama queen than Brooklyn and made Patrice's life hell while they were living together. She finally moved out in the summer to go study abroad, and Brooklyn moved in with her boyfriend about that same time. Sierra and Patrice had gotten to be good friends through some of their art classes together the past year. Despite the fact that Patrice was an undergraduate and Sierra a grad student, they got along like two peas in a pod. So, when Patrice found herself in need of a roommate, she suggested they move in together and get a two-bedroom place in West Campus. Their apartment was still fairly small, but they'd made room for Megan to crash on the couch there for several weeks after her breakup with Brad; an act of generosity for which Megan was eternally grateful.

"So, what did Renee say when you talked to her?" Sierra asked, turning back to Brooklyn's original comment."

"So, the good news is, she's coming back right after Christmas!" Brooklyn exclaimed.

"Like, just to visit for the holidays? That's kinda weird," Patrice commented.

"No, like, to stay. Apparently, France wasn't working out too good for her, so she quit the exchange program and enrolled for next semester."

"Great." Patrice wore a frown on her face, but Brooklyn didn't seem to notice.

The food came, and they all dug in. Megan devoured her pancakes. They were light and fluffy, full of chocolatey goodness, and she slathered them in butter, not syrup; just the way she liked them. Plus, they were cheap too; a tasty bargain that fit her meager dining out budget!

"How are your pancakes, Brooklyn?" she asked across the table.

"Oh my gosh, they are SO. DANG. GOOD!" Brooklyn answered. "Like, I never knew that anything vegan AND gluten free could taste this amazing!"

Patrice nudged her elbow. "See, I told you their pancakes are the best!"

Sierra licked her lips. "Mm, me, I'm in it for the queso. DE-LI-CIOUS! Here, girls, try some!" she nudged the bowl closer to the center of the table.

"No thanks," Patrice waved. "I can't do any dairy. I'm lactose intolerant, remember?"

Brooklyn also shook her head. "I don't do dairy either. I'm fine with this vegan queso of mine."

"I'll try some," Megan grabbed a chip from the bowl. "Wow! That is really something."

The Kerbey Queso had fresh guacamole and pico de gallo in it. It was so tasty that Megan had a hard time stopping after just one scoop.

"Hey, save some for me!" Sierra laughed, dunking a chip of her own into the bowl.

By the time the checks came, they were all totally stuffed. Megan's phone chirped. Seeing that it was Levi, she picked it up.
"Hey, what's up?"
"Nothin' much. Whatcha doin'?"
"Having a late dinner with my friends."

In the background, she could hear her friends talking about them.
"Who's that?" Brooklyn whispered.
"It's her boyfriend!" Sierra grinned.
"I didn't know she was dating anyone."
"It's pretty new. I haven't even gotten to meet him yet," Patrice chimed in.
"I have," Sierra whispered back. "His name's Levi and he's super cute!"

Megan's face pinked at the conversation her friends were having about her and Levi. She tried her best to ignore them and keep talking to him. When she hung up, she turned back to them.
"You guys!" she complained. "Don't talk so much while I'm on the phone!"
"Oops, my bad!" Brooklyn giggled.
"Do you need a lift back to your place?" Sierra asked as the waiter returned with their credit cards.
Megan shook her head. "No, Levi's gonna swing by and pick me up. He said he's got some books to loan me and he wants to see me, even if it's just for a little bit, since it's so late."
"Aww, that's so sweet!" Patrice cooed.
Patrice and Brooklyn headed for the ladies' room after they got up from the table, and Sierra and Megan waited outside the restaurant for them.

"So, how's everything going between you and Levi?" Sierra asked.
"It's going okay," Megan said with pursed lips.
Sierra seemed to read her mind and put her hand on Megan's shoulder. "Not every guy is like Brad, OK?"
Megan smiled. "Yeah, I know."
"Look," Sierra said. "I don't know Levi that well yet, but he seems like a really great guy. I know I only met Brad a few times, since most of the time you guys

were dating was while I was here and you two were still in Santa Fe, but I can tell you that I never got a good vibe from him."

"Really? You never said so."

"Yeah, I didn't want to burst your bubble. You were so excited that the 'office hunk' had asked you out, and especially after you had announced your engagement right before you came here, I felt like I would be overstepping if I said anything. But as soon as I met him, I had this feeling that something was off, like he wasn't telling the whole truth about himself."

"Turns out you were right," Megan said. "Gosh, I wish you'd said something."

"I did try to, that one night," Sierra admitted. "When you'd been here about two weeks, after we all went out with your co-workers and I saw him and Kimberly together. There seemed to be some strange looks going on between them, but when I mentioned it, you just brushed me off and said they were 'long-time friends' and there was nothing to worry about."

Megan sighed. "Now that you mention it, I do remember that. Man, if I had only taken you seriously then."

Sierra shook her head. "It wouldn't have mattered much. It was only a week or two later that the truth about them came out."

"Still." Megan chewed her lip. "I feel like such a schmuck for letting him lead me on like that."

Sierra patted Megan's shoulder again. "Don't be too hard on yourself. At least you've got a great guy now!"

"Yeah," Megan smiled.

"Speaking of," Sierra pointed. "I think your ride's here."

Levi's car pulled into the parking lot, and Megan climbed in eagerly. Patrice and Brooklyn emerged from the restaurant just in time to wave goodbye along with Sierra.

Patrice had a funny look on her face as Levi drove off.

"What's up?" Brooklyn asked.

"Nothin'. That guy just seemed familiar, that's all."

"Oh. Well, I didn't get a good look at him," she said.

Levi headed south from the restaurant parking lot.

"Where are we going at this late hour?" Megan asked. "Not a bar, I hope."

Levi's chuckle filled the car. "No, I've got someplace better than a bar to take you."

As he turned onto 6th street, which was known for its myriad of bars, Megan wondered if Levi was playing a joke on her. He found some street parking and they got out to walk the rest of the way to their destination.

"You still haven't said where we're headed," Megan reminded him.

"This place." Levi pointed to an old stone building with a creepy sign that read "Museum of the Weird."

"What?" Megan laughed.

"Trust me, it'll be cool."

Megan took his word for it as they passed through a quirky gift shop full of eclectic novelties. Levi stopped at the counter. "Two for the museum, please," he asked the salesclerk, who promptly exchanged his money for the tickets.

"How late does this place stay open?" Megan asked as the pair went through the turnstile.
"Until midnight," Levi answered. "Trust me, it's way better at night than during the daytime. So much creepier!"
Seeing Megan's uncomfortable expression, he said, "what? You're not scared, are you? You watched the zombie movie with me. It's no worse than that."
"Sure," Megan said, still skeptical. They entered a room with a giant King Kong head, some palm trees, and two gigantic gorilla hands.
"Hey, watch this!" Levi climbed inside one of the gorilla hands, making it look like he was being squeezed inside the fist. He pretended to scream. "He's got me, he's got me! Aaaah!"
Megan doubled over with laughter.
"Quick, take a picture!" Levi urged. Megan whipped out her phone and snapped the shot.
"Do you wanna try?" Levi asked.
"Nah, I'm good," she shook her head.

In other rooms they saw many more oddities: the skull of a "man-fish", a mummy mermaid, "bigfoot's" footprint fossils, two-headed animals and a cyclops pig, a statue of The Grinch, among other things. Megan found it all a bit odd and creepy, but it was clear that Levi really loved the place. He got a kick out of everything there and took tons of pictures. He finally got Megan to pose for one next to the life-size Dracula figurine, pretending to be the woman he was biting.

As they headed back to Levi's car, he told her, "I know that probably wasn't your favorite kind of place, but thanks for humoring me by coming along anyways."
"Ha, like I had a choice!" Megan laughed. "You dragged me over here without a car of my own to get away."
Her comment made Levi howl. "That's true, I did! You're a good sport, Megs. Next time, you can pick the date spot. Where do you like to go? The symphony? The ballet?"
"Anyplace with class," Megan replied.
"Ho, ho!" Levi whooped again. "Guess that was called for."
"Honestly, though," Megan continued, "my first choice is really just someplace quiet with lots of books to read, maybe some coffee to drink."
"Barnes and Noble it is, then."
"Not a bad idea!" Megan grinned. "But I like the library just fine too."
"Good, cuz that's free, and I won't have to feel like I'm cheating on my

workplace." More laughter ensued from both of them over that quip. "C'mon, Megs, I'll take you home."

When they reached Megan's place, Levi had a question to ask her. "By the way, I was wondering if you had any plans this weekend."
"Why? Hoping we can spend the whole time curled up in the corner of Yarborough Library with our books?"
"Actually, I'm headed to visit my parents this weekend, for Christmas. I was wondering if you'd like to come with me."
Megan froze. *This is too soon!* she thought. "I... I don't know, Levi," she began. Levi tried to assuage her. "I know we haven't been hanging out that long. I just thought, what with your family being in Santa Fe and all, you might like to be around another family for the holiday. But I dunno," he backed off. "Maybe you've got plans with Sierra already, or something."
"No, actually, her parents are meeting her in Cabo. They rented some villa there for a week to have a family vacation there. She leaves tomorrow. And Patrice is heading down to San Antonio to see her folks," she added, "so I'll actually be all alone. Maybe," she gulped, "maybe some company might be good for me."
"Awesome! My parents will be totally cool with it, I know. A-and I don't have to call you my 'girlfriend' to them, or anything, like, if you don't want me to," Levi stammered, suddenly nervous.
"Am I your girlfriend, Levi?" Megan looked up at his eyes, which had darkened from a brilliant blue into a deep shade of navy in the dim light from the streetlamps.
Now it was Levi's turn to gulp. "Well, I mean, I'd really like you to be my girlfriend. If you want to be."
Megan smiled. There was something reassuring in Levi's sweet, silly nature that made her want to trust him. "Yes, I'd like that," she told him.
"Really? I mean, whew!" he let out a sigh of relief. "I've been wanting to ask you that for like, a week now, but I couldn't seem to get up the nerve."
"I'm not sure I would have said 'yes' a week ago," she admitted. "Frankly, I'm not even sure I would have said 'yes' two minutes ago."
"Well if you're not sure--"
"I'm sure," Megan interrupted him. She put her hands on his shoulders and drew him close to her until their faces were an inch apart. Closing her eyes, she melted as his lips pressed onto hers and his arms wrapped her in his embrace. The sweetness of their encounter lasted but a moment before he released her again.
"Goodnight, Levi," Megan bid him as she headed towards the stairs.
"Goodnight, Megan Vasquez," Levi echoed with a look of pure adoration on his face.

Chapter 8

The next day, Sierra called Megan from the airport while she waited to board her flight to Mexico. Megan filled her in on her date the night before, as well as Levi's invitation.

"I just can't believe you're already going to meet his family!" Sierra gushed.

"I know. I'm pretty nervous about it," Megan admitted.

"Puleeze," Sierra drawled, "they're gonna love you. When Brad dumped you back in September, I never expected you'd already get another boyfriend by Christmas. Meanwhile, I'm still sitting here single. I've had nothing but a string of bad first dates for months now."

"Do I detect a hint of jealousy?" Megan teased.

"*Chica*, if anyone deserves to be happy, it's you. Believe me when I say, I'm incredibly happy for you. But when you're throwing the bouquet at your wedding, make sure to send it my way; I need some good luck in the love department!"

Megan laughed. "A lady's imagination is very rapid; it jumps from admiration to love, from love to matrimony, in a moment. I knew you would be wishing me joy."

Now it was Sierra's turn to laugh. "Are you quoting from *Pride and Prejudice* again?"

"Guilty as charged," Megan grinned. "But really, let's not make this any bigger of a deal than it is. I'm meeting his family, not getting engaged."

"Yet." Sierra pointed out. "Just don't blow it with this one, okay? I can already tell that he's a great catch."

"I didn't blow it with the last one either," Megan retorted.

Sierra sighed. "I know. I phrased that badly, I'm sorry. *He's* the one who blew it, not you. You deserve so much better than Brad. That's why I'm praying everything works out for you and Levi."

"Thanks, I appreciate it," Megan smiled again. "Hope you have a safe flight and have an amazing time with your *familia* in Cabo."

They hung up the phone. Megan felt a wave of envy wash over her. Sierra's family could afford to take vacations at exotic destinations like Cabo San Lucas. Her parents were well-off, and Sierra had never needed a job to help pay the bills or get through school. Megan's dad, on the other hand, had worked multiple jobs to make ends meet, and by the time Megan was in high school, she was working part-time too to help out. Her grandparents had set aside some money in an account for her before they died, so that she could go to school. That money, coupled with scholarships and the income from her part-time job, ensured that she graduated from the University of New Mexico with minimal debt. Megan had never been on any vacations, except driving to Colorado to visit her cousins a few times.

In fact, except for the places she'd been for work and school, this was the first time she'd been anywhere else besides home or to visit family. She began to look forward to her weekend getaway with Levi.

The Enchanted Moon was closed on Christmas Eve, but Megan still had to work her other job at Hobby Lobby. Luckily, they closed early, so as soon as Megan got off at five-thirty, Levi picked her up from the store. She came out wheeling the small overnight bag she'd brought with her.
"Ready to go?" he asked as she hopped into the passenger seat.
"So ready! But I'm also starving, too."
"I figured you would be." He handed her a grocery bag. "Hope it's okay, I got tacos this time. Take your pick from the selection; I got a variety."
"Awesome! You're the best."
Levi grinned. "I try to be."
Megan picked out one with beef brisket and avocados in it, and sank her teeth in. "Mmm, this is amazing!" she exclaimed through the mouthful of food. She swallowed. "Where'd you get these from?"
"They're from Torchy's Tacos."
"I've heard great things about that place, but I've never been," Megan admitted. "Growing up in a Mexican family, I've learned to be a bit picky about the kinds of taco joints I go to. Too many advertise well but aren't up to snuff. This one is, though. Mm!" she took another huge bite of the taco, savoring the acidic, herby flavor of the cilantro and tomatillo sauce.
"Eat as much as you want," Levi told her, "I already had a few."
Megan's eyes widened as she looked at how many were still in the bag. "How many did you buy?"
"I thought we should try them all, so I got two of each kind."
"Jeepers, you must have thought I'd be really hungry!"
"Either that, or I just felt really hungry myself at the time," Levi laughed. "Don't worry, if we have any leftovers, they'll be gone in an instant. My brothers and sister love tacos, and there aren't too many good places around Spring where you can get them."

"Tell me more about your family," Megan said.
"Well, let's see," Levi began, "I'm the third of five kids. My sister Abby is married; she and her husband had a baby three months ago. Then there's Daniel. He spends about three-fourths of the year doing ministry work at our village in the Dominican Republic. When he's home on leave, he helps manage the store and do inventory for my parents, does all the bookkeeping, that sort of thing. Next is me--"

"The middle child," Megan interjected.
"Yes--the middle child," Levi smiled. "After me are my younger brothers Jon and Mike, twins who are both still in High School."
"You must feel so lucky having grown up in a big family," Megan said.
"What about you? Do you have any siblings?"
Megan shook her head. "Nope. I'm an only-child. My mom and dad married in a hurry-- you know, shotgun-wedding style-- and well, they didn't get along too great after that. They fought all the time when I was little, about money, about my mom's drinking and smoking habits, her unwillingness to get a job…"
"Sounds rough," Levi sympathized.
"It was. She tried her best to be a good mom, I know that, but she was always a bit too immature. Didn't have a great work-ethic. Not like my dad, at least. She spent most of the day watching TV and smoking, then at night she would go out to party with her friends. Over time, she became an alcoholic. Then she found herself a new boyfriend. She left me and my dad when I was ten."
"Oh, Megan, I'm so sorry!"
"Yeah, me too." A lone tear escaped Megan's eye. "I haven't seen her since. She does call me about once a year to ask how I'm doing, for what it's worth."
"Not very much, in my book," Levi frowned. "She should have been there for you."
"She's not all bad," Megan tried to defend. "She did get me interested in reading; used to take me to the library to get books often. You know, before things got really bad. So, there's that, at least."
"What about your dad?" Levi asked.
"Hardest worker you'll ever find. Sweetest man too," Megan asserted. "He came from a big, big, family. I have lots of cousins on that side, and my grandparents lived close by. They helped out a lot, especially after Mom left. They even moved in with us for a while, until their health issues made it hard for my dad to care for them. So, they moved over to his brother's house instead, and lived there until they died. My dad works for a construction company, but he always had at least one other job on the side, always worked long hours to make sure there was enough food on the table and bills got paid. My mom left us with a massive amount of credit card debt, but he took care of that as soon as he could, never wanted us to be in debt for anything, not even our car or our house. The house my mom wanted was way too big for what my parents could really afford; they only bought it because she insisted on it. As soon as she left, we downsized to a much smaller place that my dad could pay off quickly."
"He sounds like a really smart guy, your dad," Levi commented.
"Yeah, he is," Megan smiled. "I hope you'll get to meet him sometime."
"I'd love that."

They were cruising along Highway 290 by now. Levi turned up the radio. The radio was set to a station playing Christmas music, which was nice. Megan bobbed her head to the jazzy rendition of "Jingle Bells Rock" that was playing.

Suddenly, the song finished, and "Feliz Navidad" came on next. Megan groaned.
"What, you don't like this one?" Levi asked.
"Nope," she answered. "It just screams Mexican-stereotype to me. It's really popular in the touristy areas of New Mexico. All the stores and local bands seem to play it non-stop at Christmas time. I get so sick of it."
"We can change the channel," Levi said. He flipped the switch over to the country station, where Luke Combs' "Hurricane" was playing.
"Much better," Megan nodded. She began humming along with the song.
"So, you like country music, then?" Levi asked.
"Yeah, I do."
"Same," he said. "My whole family does."
"My dad loves country music too. He's a big George Strait fan."
"An old-school classic country fan; my kinda guy," Levi nodded in approval.
"I like him too," Megan said, "but I kinda prefer some of the younger artists. You know, Brad Paisley, Taylor Swift, Luke Combs."
"How about Garth Brooks, Reba McEntire, Tim McGraw, Kenny Chesney?" Levi suggested.
"Yeah, I like all of them too," Megan agreed.

After the Luke Combs song, an old Jimmy Dean hit came on. Megan joined Levi in singing along with the lyrics. Megan had always loved that song, probably because of the singer comparing his heart to an "open book". Their impromptu karaoke session continued for some time with the next several country hits that came on in succession. After a while, Megan grew sleepy and dozed off. She awoke to Levi's hand gently tapping her shoulder. She looked up and realized they were parked in the driveway of a two-story house with wood siding and gingerbread trim. Multi-colored lights and white icicle lights strung from the roof and windows, along with cute candy decorations and a lighted Santa in the yard, enhanced the illusion that they had arrived at a real-life gingerbread house.
"We're here," Levi told her. The sound of their car doors alerted the residents inside, who promptly came out to greet them. A woman who could only be Levi's mother readily embraced Megan.
"Megan, it's so good to meet you! Merry Christmas!"
"Merry Christmas to you, too!" Megan blushed at the warm familiarity, already liking Levi's mom.
"I'm Diana Whittaker," she introduced herself, "and this is my husband, Steve. Welcome to our home!"
"Thank you!" Megan replied, taking Steve's offered handshake.
Steve and Diana each hugged their son next before ushering them inside.
Levi's brothers were seated on the sofa, watching Home Alone, but they rose to greet Megan and Levi. Big bear-hugs and a couple of noogies were exchanged between the four brothers. Levi introduced Megan to the twins, Mike and Jon,

both of whom shared Levi and their dad's brown hair and ruddy good looks. Levi's oldest brother, Daniel, whose blond hair resembled their mother's, was a good deal handsome too, though his vibrant blue eyes and glasses reminded Megan more of Levi than either of his parents. Perhaps they had a grandparent with blue eyes, Megan thought.

Diana offered Megan some hot cocoa and fresh gingerbread cookies.
"Thank you so much, Mrs. Whittaker," Megan replied.
"Please, call me 'Diana'," she insisted.
"And call me 'Steve' too," her husband chimed in as he stirred the hot chocolate before handing it to her.
"Tell us more about how you met," Diana urged. "Levi said something about meeting at the library?"
Megan filled them in on their chance encounter when the rain had driven her indoors at the library, then continued on to tell about their meeting again at the art museum, and their continued friendship after that."
"I think it's more than just friendship," Diana's eyes twinkled, causing Megan's cheeks to turn pink.
"Well, yes, we did just agree to be boyfriend and girlfriend," she allowed.
Diana glanced around the corner to ensure that Levi was out of earshot. He seemed preoccupied watching the movie with his brothers. Diana turned back to Megan. "I meant this is the first time he's brought anyone home for us to meet."
"You mean, you never met his last girlfriend?"
Diana shook her head. "He was with her for almost a year, but they always seemed to have such a tumultuous relationship. He called me often, saying she had threatened to break up with him, or that she was calling it 'quits', but then she would always come back to him a day or two later and beg to make up, or pretend like nothing had ever happened. She seemed like a troubled sort of girl. Steve and I offered Levi to bring her here when he would come to visit. We thought maybe we could offer her some counseling-- Steve's a pastor, you know."
Megan nodded.
Diana continued, "but Levi never wanted to bring her around. I suspect maybe he was in the relationship for reasons *other* than liking this girl's personality. But anyways..." Diana waved her hand to change the subject, "Levi's spoken of you often since you two met a few weeks ago. I can already tell; he thinks you're something special."
Megan's cheeks were flaming hot by now. "Really?" Her heart started pounding like an African tribal drum, so loud she thought Diana and Steve must have been able to hear it resounding in the kitchen. But they seemed quite nonplussed. Not for the first time, Megan wondered if things were moving too fast between her and Levi. She had never once met Brad's parents, nor he her dad, even though they'd been together for eight months.

Megan took her mug of hot chocolate and the plate of cookies into the living room. Levi looked up from the couch and beamed at her. He quickly scooched over to make room for her. His oldest brother sat on the other side of him, while the twins were occupying the two recliners. Diana and Steve joined the family, cozying up on the loveseat together. The movie continued to play in the background.

"How was the service tonight, Dad?" Levi asked.

"Oh, it was good," Steve replied. "Pretty packed, as usual. Lots of our regular attenders, plus a fair number of guests. People always seem to find time to come to church on Christmas Eve."

Megan chimed in. "So sorry we couldn't be there ourselves, Mr. Whittaker."

Steve chuckled. "I told you, you can call me 'Steve'. Don't worry about formalities here," he reassured her. "And I understand, you had to work today, Levi said. What is it that you do again?"

"Well, sir, I'm a data analyst, but I'm between jobs in that field at the moment. I'm currently working at a coffee shop and a craft store in the meantime to make ends meet," Megan told him.

"That can't be easy, juggling two jobs, and with a new boyfriend, to boot. I commend you," Steve said.

"How do you find time for anything else?" Diana asked.

"Levi's been very flexible," Megan answered. "We squeeze in dates after I get off work, or on days when I'm off from one of my jobs. One time, Levi even came to the coffee shop and helped me." She told them how Levi put his expertise from working at the family store to good use, helping her make the drinks when the espresso machine broke, and then fixing the machine. Her boss, Duke, had been grateful when he heard all Levi had done.

"I'm proud of you, son," Steve nodded, "helping a 'damsel in distress.' You always did good work for me when you were at home. You know you can always come back to work for me again, anytime you decide you want to."

Levi smiled. "Thanks, Dad, but I'm pretty happy at the library for right now."

The movie was getting to the best part, when Kevin McCallister rigs up his house with booby traps in anticipation of the burglars, who walk right into each and every trap. Conversation ceased for a bit so they could all enjoy the movie. Just as the bad guys were being hauled off to jail, Megan's phone rang. It was her dad.

"Sorry, I gotta take this," she apologized.

"Go right ahead," Diana offered.

Megan stepped out onto the back deck for privacy.

"Hey, Dad," she picked up the call.

"How are you doing, *Mija*? Merry Christmas!"

Megan smiled. "Merry Christmas to you too, Dad."

"Did you make it out to Spring okay?" Megan had told her dad previously about the trip with Levi.

"Yeah, we're here with Levi's parents and brothers, watching Home Alone."
"Good. I miss having you here with me this year. It doesn't feel like Christmas without you."
"I hope you aren't spending the holiday by yourself!" Megan chided.
"Of course not. I went to Christmas Eve mass tonight, and tomorrow I'm going over to Miguel's house for Christmas Brunch," Mr. Vasquez said. Miguel was one of his brothers, who lived close by.
"Good. Say 'hi' to *Tío* Miguel and *Tía* Victoria and all my cousins for me."
"I will," her dad promised. "So, how do you like Levi's family?"
"Everyone is so nice, Dad! I've been here less than an hour and I already feel right at home," Megan told him.
"Good, good." There was a hesitation in Mr. Vasquez' voice that made Megan question him.
"Dad? What is it?"
"Uh, it's nothing, *Mija*. I'm sure they're good people. I just wonder if...I dunno, maybe you're moving rather quickly with this new boyfriend of yours. I don't want to see you get hurt again."
His comment struck a chord with Megan. "Yeah, I know, Dad, me either. I almost said 'no' when Levi asked me to come. After all, I've only known him less than a month, and we just agreed to be boyfriend and girlfriend. But he seems so genuine, and well, I didn't want to hurt his feelings. Plus, the idea of being alone on Christmas kinda sucked." Megan bit back the tears that threatened to spill over. "I miss you, Dad!"
"I miss you too, baby girl."
"Dad, I--"
She was interrupted by a sudden groaning from her dad. "Urrrgh, uh. Excuse me," he said.
"Are you OK, Dad?"
"It's nothing. I'm fine, *Mija*, really. I've just been having some chest pains lately. The doctor says I need to go get it checked out."
"Make sure you do that," Megan insisted.
"Of course! I've got an appointment right after Christmas."
"Don't put it off, okay?"
"I won't."
"Alright. I love you, Dad," Megan said.
"I love you too, *Mija*. Have a good time with your boyfriend and his family."
"Thanks, Dad."

The movie was over when Megan stepped back inside. She shivered from having been outside without her coat.
"Hey, you look cold," Levi noticed. "Wanna come back and snuggle on the couch some more? I'll warm you up."
"Thanks, but I'm kinda tired. I think I'll turn in for the night."
"Of course," Diana stepped in. "Let me show you to your room." She showed

Megan to a room upstairs at the end of the hall. It was sweetly furnished with a white sleigh bed, matching dresser and nightstands, and the walls were covered in a pink and green floral wallpaper.

"This used to be my daughter Abby's room when she lived at home. You'll meet her tomorrow. She and her husband are coming over with my granddaughter to celebrate Christmas with us. Now, just let me know if there's anything you need. There's an extra blanket in the closet if you get cold. Bathroom's down the hall, second door to the left."

"Thank you so much, Diana," Megan smiled.

"You're welcome, dear. We're so happy to have you with us."

Levi stopped by her doorway just as his mom left. "Just wanted to make sure you have everything you need," he said.

"Everything is perfect, thanks. Your family is so wonderful, Levi!"

He smiled back. "Yeah, I got pretty lucky in that department. Well, hope you have a good night!" Levi leaned closer, using the doorway for support. Megan closed her eyes as Levi gently kissed her, letting her lips linger on his and savoring the tenderness between them. *If only every moment in life was as wonderful as this one!* she thought.

"Goodnight, Levi."

"Night, night. Hope Santa Claus brings you what you want for Christmas," he winked.

Megan blushed. "I think maybe he already has."

Levi gave her another quick peck before walking down the hall to his own room.

Chapter 9

Megan awoke to the smell of bacon and other wonderful things cooking downstairs. She dressed quickly in a red long-sleeve t-shirt and jeans, pulling half of her hair back in a barrette. Diana and Steve were already downstairs. Diana was hard at work cooking something wonderful on the stove, while Steve set the table and made coffee and tea.
He looked up from the silverware he was putting on the table when Megan entered the room.
"Good morning, Megan! Did you sleep well?" he asked.
"Very well," she answered. "The bed was so comfortable; I could have slept for a thousand years. If not for the smell of that bacon that woke me up, I think I would still be sound asleep."
Diana laughed. "Well you're the first one up, besides us. Levi and his brothers usually sleep late when they are all home on vacation. Do you like to cook?"
Megan nodded.
"Good," Diana said. "You can help me make the Toad in the Hole."
"The what?" The look on Megan's face showed she must have been thinking they were going to eat actual toads. This made Diana laugh again, before she explained what it was.
"It's sausage baked in Yorkshire pudding. My grandmother was from England, and she used to serve it all the time when I was growing up. It's become a family favorite." She put Megan to work browning the sausages on the stove, while she finished prepping the pan. She pulled the batter from the fridge where it had been resting. "Okay, let's put the sausages into this pan," Diana directed, "then we pour the batter over it and bake it."
"It sounds so easy!" Megan exclaimed.
"It is! If you like it, I'll give you the recipe," she said.
They got the pan into the oven just as the doorbell rang.
"That'll be Abby and Chad," Diana said. "Steve, would you get it?"

Steve soon returned with a blonde woman in her late twenties or early thirties, holding a baby carrier, and accompanied by a dark-haired man who must have been her husband. Steve introduced them to Megan, while Diana promptly went to peek at her little granddaughter, who was sleeping in the carrier at the moment. Abby jumped in to help her mom get the food on the table, freeing Diana to walk to the staircase and call up.
"Boys, your sister's here! Time to get up for brunch!"
Within a few minutes, Daniel and the twins appeared, followed shortly by Levi. He was dressed comfortably in a navy sweater and jeans. His chestnut hair was

still sticking up in places. Megan itched to pat down the cowlicks and make them behave. He beamed the world's biggest smile when he saw Megan.
"Merry Christmas!"
Megan grinned too. "Merry Christmas!"
Their chorus was echoed around the dining table as the family sat down for the meal. Everything was delicious; the crispy bacon, the gooey homemade cinnamon rolls, the sweetly refreshing assorted fruit tray. But Megan's favorite was the Toad in the Hole. It reminded Megan of the Mexican chorizo and egg casserole that her *abuelita* used to make. The savory sausage, mixed with the fluffy eggs, just hit the spot, a perfect breakfast dish, in Megan's opinion. The only difference was her *abuelita's* casserole used a much spicier meat, and she usually put *jalapeño* peppers in as well.
"What do you think?" Diana asked as Megan went for a second helping of the casserole.
"It's so good!" she exclaimed. "I will definitely be taking you up on your offer for that recipe."

After breakfast, they all gathered in the living room. Steve pulled out some extra chairs, so there would be enough seats for everyone. Megan took her place beside Levi on the sofa again. Steve began passing out the presents from under the tree. Abby and Chad's baby started crying from inside her carrier.
"I guess maybe she's hungry for her second breakfast," Abby laughed as she pulled the infant out.
"Second breakfast?" Megan asked.
"Oh sure. She already ate once at about six this morning. This girl eats like a hobbit, I swear," Abby joked. She put on an affected British accent. "Breakfast, second breakfast, elevensies, luncheon, afternoon tea, dinner, supper."
Megan laughed at her Lord of the Rings reference. "She must be the cutest hobbit I've ever seen, though," Megan cooed at the tiny babe. Little Stephanie had dark hair like her daddy, but blue eyes like her mommy. Megan thought she was just precious. Abby took her into another room to nurse her, while Steve continued handing out presents.
To Megan's surprise, there was one for her! By the look and feel of it, she guessed it must be a book.
"I'm astonished! I never expected you would have anything for me," she said. "But I didn't bring presents for any of you..."
Diana reassured her. "Don't worry, we didn't expect you to get us anything in return, but we wanted you to have something to open too. Why don't you go first?" she suggested.
Seeing no arguments from any of the others, Megan obliged. She carefully unwrapped the pretty gold foil wrapping paper, thinking perhaps she could reuse it later.
"C'mon, just rip into it!" Jon called impatiently from the other side of the room, causing Megan to flush.

"Ignore him," Levi told her. "Take your time."
Megan finally got the wrap undone and slid it carefully off the book inside. She gasped when she saw the cover. It was a beautiful, hardback illustrated edition of *Pride and Prejudice*, embellished with a gold peacock on the front. Tears began welling up in her eyes, despite her efforts to quell them.
"Levi told us that's your favorite novel, but that you'd still been borrowing a copy from the library," Diana explained. "He helped us pick that one out online for you."
"I hope you like it," Levi added.
"It's beautiful, thank you so much!" Megan said through her tears of joy.

Levi and his family took turns opening their gifts. Sometime in the middle of the exchange, Abby returned from nursing Stephanie. The baby seemed quite wide awake now, and she was happier now that she'd been fed.
"Can I hold her?" Megan asked.
"Sure!" Abby said, more than willing to get a break from holding her child. She handed little Stephanie to Megan, who began playing "Patty-Cake" with her.
"Looks like she likes you," Diana commented as Stephanie gurgled and cooed in Megan's arms.
"Do you have any nieces or nephews?" Abby asked.
Megan shook her head. "No, but I have a lot of cousins, some of whom are now married with children. There's always at least one baby or toddler to hold when I go to visit family, it seems."
"I'm sure they love you. You're a natural!" Abby complimented.
"Thank you," Megan blushed.
Levi watched with adoration at how well his niece took to Megan, and how much enjoyment she seemed to be having in holding her. Finally, little Stephanie decided she'd had enough and wanted her own mama back, so Megan handed her back to Abby.

The rest of the day was pleasant and fun. After presents, they all played cards and board games. In the afternoon, Diana laid out a self-serve buffet of cold cuts, so everyone could make their own sandwiches whenever they felt hungry enough. This allowed them to keep playing their games without too much interruption. In the evening, a full dinner was unnecessary, since they were all too full still, but she brought out popcorn and other snacks, so they could munch while they hung out.
"Wanna sit out on the deck?" Levi asked Megan.
"Sure, just lemme grab my coat first." She went upstairs to fetch it, also retrieving a small package from her overnight bag.
She met Levi outside on the back deck. He was looking at his phone, but he put it away when he saw her. "Brr, it's cold out here!" she exclaimed as she took a seat beside him on a study wooden rocking chair.
"It won't be for long." He motioned to the fire pit, which he had lit only a

minute earlier. "If we sit close, we can stay warm and still enjoy the night air." They drew their chairs close to the fire.

"I hope you're having a good time," Levi said.

"The best!" Megan answered. "I couldn't have asked for a better Christmas."

"Good," Levi smiled. "I hope I can make it just a little bit better, though. I wanted to wait until we were alone to give you this." He pulled a small velvet jewelry box from his pocket. Megan gasped in horror. "Don't worry," he reassured her. "It's not a ring."

"Whew!" she sighed. "That would be moving things a little *too* quickly."

"Agreed!" Levi laughed. "Well, go on. Open it up!"

Megan lifted the dainty lid. In the glow from the fire, she could make out the glint of a lovely gold pendant, inscribed with some writing. She held it closer to the flames so she could make it out. It was a quote from *Pride and Prejudice*, naturally.

"I declare after all, there is no enjoyment like reading!" Megan read. "How much sooner one tires of anything than of a book!"

"I thought it was perfect for you," Levi said.

"It is!" Megan couldn't help laughing though.

"What's so funny?"

"The quote is very applicable to my life, I will admit, but what's funny is that the person who said this in the book, Caroline Bingley, is someone who only pretended to like reading in order to impress the man she liked!"

Now Levi roared with laughter. "That *is* funny!" he agreed. "Had I known that I might have picked out a different quote."

"I have something for you too," Megan said. "Like you, I wanted to give it when your family wasn't around." She handed him the small package she'd hidden in her coat pocket.

He began untying the ribbon around the box. "It's not a ring, is it?" he smirked.

Megan laughed. "See for yourself."

Levi opened the box to reveal a carved bookplate stamp, with a metal seal affixed to it. The seal was custom engraved with Levi's name and initials and the Latin words "ex libris".

"I noticed you like to loan out your books," Megan said. "Now you can imprint them with your very own seal of ownership, so anyone who borrows them will remember who they belonged to and return them to you."

"It's the perfect gift for a librarian like me," Levi said. "Thank you, Megan!" He leaned towards her rocking chair and planted a kiss on her cheek.

"I'm glad you like it."

"I *love* it!" Levi emphasized. He gently turned her face towards his and kissed her lips.

Megan wasn't sure if it was the heat from the fire, or from his kiss, that made her feel so warm. Whichever the case, her heart seemed to ignite, and she found herself kissing him back with greater passion that she had known before. When they pulled back from each other, Megan's cheeks flushed and she let out a small giggle, embarrassed at her own forwardness. For a few minutes, neither one of them spoke. The air was pregnant with words unsaid, words that they didn't dare utter for fear that it was too soon to reveal the depth of their feelings. Finally, Levi suggested that they return inside, and Megan was thankful for it.

Duke had told Megan not to worry about coming in to work the day after Christmas, but she had no such luck with the craft store. They needed her there by the afternoon shift, since the day after Christmas was one of their biggest sale days, when they would clearance all the Christmas wreaths, florals, ornaments, and other holiday kitsch. Still, Levi wanted to show Megan around the town before they left. First thing in the morning, he drove her over to his family's coffee shop in the heart of Old Town Spring, Dominican Java. Daniel was already there, filling the glass case with pastries from a local bakery. Megan could smell the signature brew going in the industrial coffee machines when they walked in. They ordered some drinks. Levi wanted to give them to her on the house, knowing his parents would not mind in the least, but Megan insisted she ought to pay for them.
"The profit goes towards the villagers in the D.R.," she said, "so it wouldn't be right for me not to pay. I want to make my contribution towards your family's ministry."
Levi could not argue with her.

"How does the taste compare with Enchanted Moon?" he wanted to know.
"It's way better! I never thought there was much difference in coffee beans from one place to another, but I can really taste the velvety, nutty flavor that comes across from these. I should tell Duke to start carrying your imported coffee at Enchanted Moon; the customers would love it!"
"I'm sure my family would be most appreciative, and so would the villagers who grow it," Levi smiled.

After they finished their drinks, it was nearly time to head back to Austin, but Levi wanted to show her one more place. Across the street from the coffee shop was a tiny gift shop, called "Little Dutch Girl". Megan was enchanted the moment they walked in. The shop was filled with teacups, dishes, lace, knick-knacks, and other darling little curio items, mostly Dutch things. Megan was sorely tempted by a set of pink and purple flowered teacups and matching teapot.
"They look like something out of one of the Jane Austen books," she said. But in the end, it was an adorable creamer shaped like a cow that stole her heart. It was white, with blue flowers and a blue windmill painted on it, it had a real miniature bell hung from its neck, and it poured milk from its mouth when you tipped it. "It looks just like the one that my *abuelita* used to have," she told Levi. "I wonder whatever happened to it. I used to love when she would let me use it to pour milk into my cereal in the morning. It was just the right size to hold a

bowlful of milk, and that way the milk wasn't too heavy for me to pour by myself."

"That's such a sweet story," Levi commented. "Are you going to get it?"

Megan shook her head. "I don't think so." The sad expression on her face told Levi she wanted it, in truth, but that she didn't have enough money in her budget for such a luxury item.

"I'm going to buy it for you," he declared.

"But you've already gotten me a Christmas present!" she reminded him.

"I know. This is a souvenir of your time here in Spring, and a memento to remind you of your *abuelita*."

"Thank you, Levi!" she hugged him, right there in the middle of the store.

With the ceramic cow safely wrapped for the journey, they hit the road and made good time back to Austin. Diana had packed them some lunch to eat on the way, so they didn't need to stop except for five minutes to get gas along the way.

Levi dropped Megan off at the craft store in time for her shift to start.

"Thank you again, for everything, Levi. I had a wonderful time."

"So did I." She leaned over to give him a quick kiss goodbye. As she pulled away, he grabbed her back and kissed her again, longer this time. His phone, sitting in the cupholder to charge, vibrated. "I gotta go to work, Levi," Megan reminded him.

"I know," he whispered, still holding her. "Just one more minute." They kissed some more. Levi's phone went off again.

"Don't you need to check that?"

"Naw, it's probably just my mom checking to make sure we got back okay," he shook his head and kept on enjoying Megan's lips. Finally, when Megan knew she would be late for her shift if she didn't go, Levi released her reluctantly.

"Talk to you soon, Megs," he said, holding onto her hand until the last moment.

"You too," she smiled, finally shutting the car door afterwards. Levi continued to watch her until she entered the building.

Megan had to work a lot the next few days, but she still came by the library every chance she got, whether between her two jobs, or at the end of the day when she finally left the craft store. The library staff got used to seeing her, and she began to feel like they were a sort of second family. Loretta was always warm and affectionate. Besides calling her "honey", she had taken to giving Megan a hug whenever she came in. Bart, too, was always friendly and agreeable. He usually gave Levi extra time on his breaks so he could spend time with Megan, and the other assistant librarians didn't seem to mind picking up the slack.

The week flew by.

"Hey *Chica*," Sierra said over the phone on Friday.

"Hey, yourself! How was the trip to Mexico?" Megan asked.
"It was great! I actually met somebody while we were there."
"You're kidding!"
"Nope!" Sierra replied. She told how when she and her family were out on a boating excursion, she accidentally fell overboard. Their guide, a handsome young man by the name of Carlos, dived in the water to rescue her. After that, she kept running into him at the resort, where he was the director of guest excursions, and they hit it off.
"Are you sure you didn't fall off that boat on purpose?" Megan asked skeptically.
Sierra laughed. "Honest to goodness!"
"A vacation fling, huh? I never would have guessed it of you."
"Me either," Sierra agreed. "We exchanged numbers and social media though, and we're planning to keep in touch, so who knows that might happen down the road." Changing the subject, she said, "Hey, a bunch of us are going to the big New Year's Eve party over at Brooklyn's dorm tomorrow night. Wanna come?"
Megan bit her lip. Ringing in the New Year with Brooklyn and her friends, even if that included Sierra and Patrice, sounded less than appealing. "I dunno, Sierra, I was kinda thinking about spending the evening with Levi, since Hobby Lobby closes early."
"Bring him along!" Sierra suggested. "Patrice says she's dying to meet him, and I think I ought to get to know him a bit better myself, since you two have already been to visit his parents together."
"Sierra! It's not like that," Megan chided.
"Haha, I know, but now that you two have made it 'official' I think you owe it to me as your best friend to bring your boyfriend around to hang out with us once in a while. Besides, when was the last time you went to a party of any kind?"
"Okay, okay, I give in. What time is the party?"

Levi was texting on his phone when Megan met him outside the library after work that evening. He had a frown on his face. He put the phone away and smiled when he saw Megan.
"Everything okay?" she asked.
"Yeah, everything is fine," he reassured her. "Ready to go?"
Megan nodded. Levi had also just gotten off work for the day, so the two of them were going to drive over to Megan's place for some dinner together. In the car, Megan invited him to come to the New Year's Eve party the next night.
"Sure, sounds good! Just text me the address and the time, and I'll be there."
They had a lovely meal together. Levi cooked spaghetti and meatballs, and Megan swore her tiny kitchen had never smelled so good before. She made the salad and the garlic bread, and they devoured all the food quick as lightning. As they cleared the dishes, Levi's phone beeped. He frowned again as he read the text and typed back a reply. Then he returned to helping with the dishes. His

phone went off several times while they loaded the dishwasher and scrubbed the pans, but he ignored it.

"Aren't you going to check that?" Megan asked as his phone beeped for the seventh or eighth time.

"I'm with you right now," Levi answered, "and I refuse to be bothered by anyone else." He pulled Megan into his arms and kissed her soundly. His kiss awakened something in Megan, a brazen desire to do more, to feel more. She responded to it by teasing his lips gently with tiny kisses. He sighed with pleasure as she bit down gently on his lower lip. Scooping her up as if she were a feather, he set her down on the freshly wiped kitchen counter, urging her to continue their passion. He traced her back from the shoulders down, resting his hands on her waist. Meanwhile, Megan allowed her hands to roam free in his thick hair, playing with all those messy pieces that liked to stick up, just as she'd been longing to do. She scooted her bottom forward and pressed her chest into his. Levi knew if they went any further, he wouldn't be able to control himself. He pulled back from her and cleared his throat. "We should, uh, stop now, I think." Megan nodded, coming back to reason. She knew it wouldn't be wise for either of them to continue too.

"It's getting late," she said. "Do you want me to walk you to your car?"

"Nah, I'll be alright," Levi shook his head. "I'll see you tomorrow, Megs." He allowed himself a kiss on her cheek, but no more. Then he waved goodbye and left her apartment. Megan, still sitting on her countertop, let out a big sigh. *Don't play with fire, Megan,* she told herself, *you might get burned.*

Chapter 10

Promptly at closing time, Megan raced to the back room of the craft store and hung up her work vest. Underneath, she'd worn her favorite jeans and the black polyester v-neck that Levi had liked her in on their first "real" date. Sierra and Patrice picked her up this time, to take her to the party. Levi didn't get off until a few hours later, so he would meet her there, he said.
"You're wearing that?" Sierra raised an eyebrow as Megan hopped in the backseat.
"What's wrong with it? You guys picked it out for me last time. Levi said I looked good in it."
Patrice whipped around from the front passenger seat to look at her. "Yeah, but that was for, like, a coffee date. Girl, this is New Year's Eve! You need to look a little more…"
"Spectacular," Sierra filled in for her. She and Patrice both had on glitzy cocktail dresses, tons of makeup, and sparkly jewelry. "We've got time, right?" Patrice nodded in agreement. "Then it's settled," Sierra stated. "We're taking you back to our place and giving you a makeover."

Megan had no choice. She was her friends' Barbie doll for the night. Patrice was closer in size to Megan than Sierra was, so it was from her closet that they borrowed a slinky gold lamé sheath. Despite it having long sleeves, it was still way sexier than anything Megan usually wore, and the shortness of it made her feel conspicuous. Still, the girls insisted that Megan looked fabulous in it. They found some gold sandals that fit Megan's feet well enough, and when they added a long gold necklace, big gold earrings, and a gold cuff, she had so much bling on her she looked like she had been kissed by Midas. Sierra, who was the master of the "smoky eye", did Megan's makeup. When she looked in the mirror at herself, Megan thought she was scarcely recognizable.
"Levi is gonna be knocked dead by you, girl!" Patrice exclaimed.
Sierra nodded. "Mmhm! You look like a million bucks, *Chica*!"
"I feel like I'm wearing that much too. Look how much you've weighed me down with all this stuff!"
"Nah, it's just a little glitz!" Patrice dismissed.
"You two must be my fairy godmothers."
Sierra and Patrice laughed.
"Well, we've done our best," Sierra said. "Now, 'off to the ball' with you!"

The three glittering divas made their way over to one of the campus' biggest co-ed dormitories, where a rip-roaring party was already underway in the main lobby. Loud music was playing from the DJ booth, and a disco ball hung from the ceiling flashed lights in every direction. They managed, after some time, to locate Brooklyn, who was dancing with her boyfriend Kurt.

"Hey, you guys made it!" she stopped dancing to hug them all. "Kurt and I were just saying how great it would be if y'all came."

"I told you we would," Patrice said.

"Guess who's here?" Brooklyn asked. She tapped another girl on the shoulder, who stopped dancing and turned to join them.

"You remember Renee, right?" Brooklyn gestured to her friend. As the slender brunette in the red cocktail dress shook their hands, Megan thought she seemed rather familiar. Then she remembered: she had met Renee only once, shortly after arriving in Austin. Renee had been upset about a fight she'd had with her boyfriend and gone on a drunken rant at the bar they were all hanging out at. The next thing she'd heard, Renee had left for her study abroad in France, freeing her old roommates to seek their current living arrangements.

"It's nice to see you again," Megan said politely.

"Likewise. I don't remember you, though. What's your name again?"

"Megan," she replied through gritted teeth.

Brooklyn went back to dancing with Kurt, leaving the rest of them to make small talk with Renee.

"So, I heard you just came back from France. Is that right?" Megan tried her best to be friendly.

"Yeah," Renee said. "Like, Paris is totally awesome. 'City of Love' and all that, and there's a lot of fun to be had there and down in the Riviera on the weekends. I guess I got bored with the whole 'art program' thing, since I don't speak French. Like, at all."

"Really?" Megan said, trying to sound surprised.

"Yah. Anyways, it was a bit of a drag, cuz they wanted me to copy all these old paintings and sculptures from some museum called 'The Luuve', or something like that."

Megan groaned inwardly at her bad pronunciation of "Louvre", and her obvious lack of knowledge regarding anything of class and substance.

Renee continued, "and since I was missing my poor Witty-- that's my boyfriend-- I decided to quit the program early and come home."

"Didn't you two break up?" Patrice asked. "That's what I heard from Brooklyn."

"Well, she's mistaken. Witty is very much still my boyfriend. We've been together this whole time. It's been terribly painful, being separated from him these past months, and a long-distance relationship is so trying. I think he's still a little mad at me for going so far away. He should be coming tonight, though. I texted him about the party so he could come. I've been missing him something terrible. I've only seen him once since I got back. He went to East Texas for Christmas to visit his family, and then--oh wait, here he is now!" Renee trotted off in her skimpy red dress to greet her boyfriend. Megan turned to look. She wasn't sure what she expected to see, but she certainly didn't expect to see someone who looked like the spitting image of Levi. No wait-- it *was* Levi! He had slicked his chestnut hair back with gel, and he looked more handsome than ever all dressed up in a dark blue shirt and black chinos, but it was unmistakably him."

Megan couldn't believe her eyes as Renee splayed her arms around him and gave him a smooch.

"Levi?" the words escaped her lips as she stood there gaping.

Levi saw Megan over Renee's shoulder and immediately pushed the girl back. He looked positively astonished.

Megan didn't know what to believe. All she knew was that Renee had claimed this man to be her boyfriend, had kissed him in front of everyone, and he hadn't pushed her back until he saw Megan standing there. She strode past him out the door, tears overflowing from her eyes.

"Wait! It's not what it looks like," Levi insisted.

"Witty, where are you going?" Renee yanked on his arm, stopping him from following Megan. "You just got here. C'mon, let's dance!"

Levi jerked his arm back from her. "I told you not to call me that," he said angrily. "Why are you here? I said in my texts that I wasn't going to meet you."

"Then why did you come to the party, like I invited you to?" Renee asked.

"Wait, what?" Levi did a turnabout to face Renee.

"The party, in Jester dorms, like I mentioned," Renee was irritated now.

"This is Jester? Megan only gave me an address."

"Wait, you were supposed to meet *her*?" Her face went from irritated to livid.

In the background, Patrice and Sierra were watching this whole exchange.

"This is some drama," Sierra commented. "Too bad we don't have any popcorn."

"Totally," Patrice said with a hint of sarcasm. "I'd met Renee's 'Witty' before, as she calls him, but I had no idea he'd turn out to be the same guy as Megan's Levi."

"We'd better find Megan," Sierra said. "She'll be in a bad state right now, and she has no car."

Patrice nodded, glancing over at Brooklyn. The redhead seemed oblivious to everything that was happening, still dancing with her boyfriend. Knowing Brooklyn wouldn't miss them, Patrice and Sierra left the party to look for their friend.

They found Megan walking towards Martin Luther King Jr. Blvd, no doubt hoping to catch a bus.

"Hey," Sierra called as they caught up to her. She immediately pulled Megan into a big hug. Patrice joined in, wrapping her arms around them both as Megan sobbed.

"We saw what happened. That was crazy back there!" Patrice said.

"I knew Renee was a pretty big witch, but Levi…" Sierra shook her head. "I never would have expected that he'd be two-timing on you like that."
"Yeah, I thought those two had broken up before Renee went to France. I guess they kept it all going this whole time, long-distance."
"Sorry, guys, but I don't really wanna talk about it right now," Megan sniffed.
"You're right. Let's just get you home, *Chica*," Sierra patted her on the back. They went to where Sierra's car was parked. "Do you want some company tonight? You could crash at our place if you want to."
"Thanks, that would be great, actually."

Renee continued to chew out Levi. "After all we've been through together, I come home to find out you've gotten yourself another woman while I was away? Some hood rat from who knows where?"
Levi pointed a finger straight at her face. "That's quite enough of that. Megan is a fine woman, and I will not stand for you slinging racial slurs around about her. Furthermore," he continued, "I've told you time and again, we are not together anymore. Stop stalking me."
"How can you say we aren't together anymore?" Renee pleaded, following Levi outside to the courtyard. "I came home from France for you. I love you!"
Levi shook his head. "No, you don't. I made it quite clear before you left that I was through with all your games, always breaking up with me anytime we had a spat, then begging to get back together again the next day. I've had enough of your drama. When you broke up with me just before your trip, I told you that we were breaking up for real that time, for good."
"But I thought that was just our way of showing each other our passion," Renee insisted. "I break up with you, you break up with me, then we make up and act like nothing happened."
"Yeah, well, I was done with all that. I *am* done with all that," he emphasized. "Besides, even if there was a chance that I still thought we were together, you made it clear you had moved on to greener pastures on the other side of the pond."
"What do you mean?" Renee asked.
Levi scowled. "Oh, don't play dumb! I saw the pictures of you on Facebook. Pictures of you and a number of other men, hanging on each other, posing for selfies cheek-to-cheek, even kissing."
"That's," Renee struggled to explain, "that's just how French men are, you know. They're very affectionate people. Everyone there greets each other with at least two kisses on the cheek."
"These weren't just kisses on the cheek, Renee."
"Okay, okay, so I had a couple of flings," she finally admitted. "But only because I was missing you so much! They didn't mean anything; they were just a stand-in while we were apart. You're still the one I love!"
Levi shook his head, his gaze narrowed. He scoffed. "You don't even know the meaning of the word 'love', Renee. I moved on. I'm with Megan now. Accept it."

"So, this is your revenge against me, then?" Renee was mad again. "You saw some stupid pictures on Facebook, so you went out and slept with someone else to get even with me?"

"No, Renee, that's not how it was. I met the sweetest, kindest girl, who shares my love of books, has the same taste in music, in art, in so many other things that I do. And you know what? I fell in love with her." He began walking away from Renee again, then he turned back. "And for your information, we haven't slept together yet either. I don't plan on repeating the mistakes I made when I was with you. The next woman I sleep with will be my wife."

"Oh ho! Look who's gone all high-and-mighty! I knew the second you told me you were a preacher's boy that you'd get on your moral horse one of these days. You were a prude when I first met you, but I thought I'd brought you down to my level, at least. We had some fun times together, didn't we?"

"Yes, Renee, you did bring me down to your level. But I'm not that person anymore. And I don't want to see you ever again, do you hear me?"

His words stung as much as if he'd slapped Renee across the face. Tears began flowing, and she pouted. Turning on her heels, she shrieked as she stalked back to the party without him, no doubt meaning to drink and party into an oblivion to try to forget about this whole thing. There was a good chance she might not even remember it all in the morning and would try to repeat the same bull-crap nonsense again. Levi hoped not. He hoped he had gotten through to her. But now was not the time to do that. Right then, he needed to find Megan and try to salvage things with her.

Patrice was making up a bed for Megan on their couch when her phone rang. It was Brooklyn.

"Omigosh, you won't believe what happened tonight? My friend Renee said her boyfriend showed up at the party, and his *other girlfriend* happened to be there too! Then he went and told her that they weren't together anymore and that he didn't want to see her ever again. She sobbed for like, an hour straight. Then she got so drunk that she passed out in my room."

"You know what, Brooklyn," Patrice said, "I really don't want to hear about Renee and her troubles right now. I'm busy tending to that *other girlfriend*, a.k.a, his *real girlfriend*."

"What?" Brooklyn was confused.

"Look, I don't have time to explain right now, okay? I'll call you some other time." She hung up the phone.

"Who was that?" Megan asked as she returned from the bathroom, dressed in one of Sierra's t-shirts with a pair of Patrice's comfy shorts.

Patrice shook her head. "Nobody."

Sierra handed Megan a cup of tea. "I thought you could use a hot beverage to calm you down before bed."

Megan smiled over the gesture. "Thanks." As she sipped the drink, she said, "I do have one question that's been bugging me. Why did Renee call Levi 'Witty'?"
Patrice laughed. "Well, I can answer that one for you. Levi was in the same Renaissance art class as Renee and I were one semester; that's how those two met. The professor always called Levi by his last name, Whittaker. Levi, being such a jokester, eventually became known in the class as "Witty Whittaker". He took it all in stride as a class nickname, but for some reason, Renee kept calling him that long afterwards. He had begun to hate it by that time, but she wouldn't call him by his real name. In fact, I had completely forgotten that his first name was actually Levi," Patrice admitted. "That's why I never put two-and-two together that they were the same man, her Witty and your Levi."
"That makes sense," Megan agreed. "Just wish I'd seen the signs sooner." As she thought about it, she realized that Renee must have been the one who kept texting him the night before, probably even the other day too. She also recalled the photograph of them together she'd found in the glove box of his car, finally recognizing Renee as the same woman she'd met in the bar that one night. Despite his claims that he'd broken up some months prior, he hadn't thrown away the photo until after she'd found it.

Meanwhile, Levi figured that Megan would have gone home to her apartment. She wasn't answering her phone-- much as he would have expected-- so he drove over to her place to see if she could be reasoned with in-person. He knocked on the door repeatedly.
"Megan, it's me, Levi. Won't you at least talk to me?" he asked through the door. But there was no answer. From the parking lot, he could see that the lights were all off in her apartment. For all intents and purposes, she was either ignoring him and pretending to sleep, or she wasn't home. He pounded on the door some more, but to no avail. Dejected, he went home.

Megan was bleary-eyed the next morning after the sleepless night she had. Nevertheless, she showed up for work on time.
"How was your New Year's Eve?" Duke asked as he walked in the door.
"Don't ask," Megan shook her head.
"Uh oh, rough night?"
"The worst."
"Any advice I can offer?"
"Sorry, but I don't want to talk about it," Megan shook her head.
Duke felt Megan's pain. "Sorry to hear. Do you want to take the rest of the day off?" he offered.
"Thanks, but working will keep my mind off of everything," Megan said.

A while later, Sierra and Patrice came.
"Hey, girl, you sneaked out on us this morning," Patrice said.
"Yeah, we thought you would sleep in after the rough night you had," Sierra

added.

Megan shook her head. "Nope. Had to work. Didn't want to stay at my pity-party. I've spent too many hours in that place this year already." She was doing her best to put on a good show, but her friends could see that she was about to cave in to her tears at any minute.

Sierra and Patrice ordered some drinks and sat down at the bar counter so they could keep Megan company while she worked.

Despite the holiday the night before, the shop was packed that morning. Megan and Duke were kept on their toes until past noon, when the crowds finally died down.

About the time the shop thinned out, Megan got a call on her cell.

"Sorry, Duke, it's my other job," she winced.

"Go ahead, take it." Duke jabbed in the direction of the back room, where she could answer the call in privacy.

Megan returned a few minutes later with tears in her eyes. "The store let me go."

"Oh, Megan!" her friends consoled.

She sniffed. "I knew this was coming, I just didn't expect it to be so soon after the new year. I thought if I worked hard, they might keep me on for a while longer."

"Well, you needn't worry about the lost income," Duke patted her on the back. "I'm giving you a promotion: manager, with full-time hours and benefits!"

A smile broke through Megan's tears. "Really? You really are the best boss, Duke!" She gave the older man a side-hug. A question still hung in the air. "But, what about your nephew?"

"He was supposed to show up for his shift an hour ago. Do you see him here? Cuz I don't. Family or not, that boy is fired. Plus, I've a mind to hire some additional workers. My mother-in-law is still recuperating from her surgery, and I can't be in here as often as I'd like. Would either of you like a job?" he turned to Sierra and Patrice. The two friends had been complaining for the past hour about their lack of spending money. Megan knew it was because they usually blew most of their allowance on clothes, dining out, and movies, but she didn't think she ought to say that.

"Wow, Duke, that would be awesome!" Sierra exclaimed.

"Totally!" Patrice added. "We'd get to see Megan a lot more if we're here, since this girl is always working."

Megan smiled. "You guys are sweet."

Duke said, "I'm offering flexible hours, part-time. I know you've both got school to juggle as well. Just let me know your schedules and I'll work you in."

As if on cue, Keenan and Veronica waltzed through the door. "Yo, Unk, I'm here for my shift," he swaggered.

Duke scowled at his nephew's disrespectful way of talking to him. "Sorry, but you've been replaced."

"Say what?"
"You heard me. You're fired. You came to work late for the last time."
"Oh yeah? I don't need your stupid job anyways," Keenan fumed. "Good luck finding some other chumps who want to work in your lame-o coffee shop, their ears gone broke from havin' to listen to smooth jazz all day."
"As a matter of fact," Duke informed him, "I have already hired two new employees, and promoted my best worker to manager," he gestured to the three girls. Of the three, it was hard to tell who looked the smuggest.
"Well I, uh--" Keenan was flabbergasted.
"Say 'hi' to my sister for me when you get home," Duke smirked. "I'm sure she'll love to hear your explanation for why you showed up late to work again and got canned."
"Jeez, man, doing this to your own family," Keenan grumbled. Turning to Veronica, who had been pouting on the side the whole time, he said, "C'mon, let's get out of here."
She wagged her finger at him. "Uh, uh. I don't date losers who've got no job. It's bad enough you're still living with your momma. Now you can't even afford to take me out on a date! How're you gonna get another job? You dropped outta high school and never went back."
"But--" Keenan tried to interrupt.
"Your momma already threatened she was gonna throw you out if you didn't keep your job. I ain't gonna be some homeless bum's girlfriend. Uh-uh! We're finished."
Before Keenan could stop her, Veronica strutted out of the coffee shop without him.
Keenan pointed a finger at Megan. "This is your fault, you know!" Dashing out the door after his now-ex-girlfriend, he called, "Veronica! Baby, wait!"

A chorus of laughter echoed, mingling with the mellow tones of jazz that Keenan so claimed to hate.
Duke headed to the back room to grind more coffee beans.
"Well, that almost makes up for breaking up with my boyfriend last night," Megan said, her chuckle laced with bitterness. "At least I can say that Keenan and I are in the same boat in the love department right now," she said wryly.
"Hey, don't compare yourself to him! You did nothing to deserve what happened to you," Sierra told her.
A flood of emotions came racing at Megan. "It just...it just feels like Brad all over again."
"I just can't believe that Levi would be cheating on you," Sierra shook her head.
"I don't know Levi that well," Patrice said," but I sure do know Renee. That girl's crazy! I can't understand why he would still be dating her after the emotional whiplash she put him through. Are you sure that they're really still together? Maybe Renee made it all up. She can be delusional."
"You were both there," Megan reminded them. "You saw them kissing."

"I saw Renee kiss Levi. I'm not sure Levi was kissing her back," Patrice pointed out. "I'm not ready to let Levi off the hook yet," Sierra said, "but maybe you should talk to him. Find out the truth."

"I already blocked his number and deleted it from my phone," Megan said, slightly regretting her hasty actions at 2am, when she had grown tired of ignoring the five-hundredth phone call from Levi.

"Why not go to his house or the library? I'm sure you'd find him," Patrice suggested.

Megan barely had time to contemplate that thought before her phone rang again. She glanced at the caller ID. "Hmm, I don't recognize this number."

"Answer it!" Sierra urged. "Maybe it's him."

Duke returned to the front counter in time to help the next round of customers that just came in, so Megan took her call in the back room.

"Hello?"

"Is this Megan Vasquez?" an unknown woman's voice asked.

"Yes, this is she."

"I'm a nurse at St. Vincent Memorial Hospital in Santa Fe. Your father has been admitted after a heart attack."

Chapter 11

"Oh no, is my dad okay?" Megan gasped.
"Mr. Vasquez is stabilized, but his condition is critical. You were named in his medical records as next of kin," the nurse told her.
"Have the doctors said anything more regarding his condition?" Megan asked.
"Yes. Dr. Rampal recommends that he undergo an angioplasty to put in stents."
"That sounds serious."
"It is," the nurse said. "There's a chance he may not survive the procedure. But without it, there is a high likelihood of his suffering another heart attack, and this time, he may not be so lucky."
Megan choked up. "Th-thank you for telling me."
"Of course," the nurse replied. She left the number and address for the hospital.

Megan returned to the front of the coffee shop and told her friends what had happened.
"I'm sorry, Duke, I'm afraid I'm going to need to take time off from work indefinitely."
"Take all the time you need," Duke nodded.
Megan bit her lip. "I think at this point, it would be wise if I don't accept the promotion you've offered me."
"I understand," he said. "However, if you change your mind, know that the job is always on the table for you."

Megan went home right away to pack. Sierra and Patrice came along to help her. Megan didn't know how she would pay for the plane fare, but her friends took care of that as well. Sierra immediately offered up her frequent flyer miles, and Patrice promised to chip in if that wasn't enough to cover the cost.
"How can I ever repay you guys?"
Patrice placed a hand on Megan's shoulder. "Don't worry about it. I can do without eating out for the next month if I have to. Besides, we both just got new jobs."
"Yes, please help Duke take care of the coffee shop in my absence."
"It's in good hands," Sierra smiled.

Several hours later, Megan arrived in Santa Fe. She took a cab straight to the hospital from the airport. Her uncle and aunt, Miguel and Victoria, were in the room with her dad when she entered. Gabriel Vasquez was asleep in the hospital bed.
Megan's aunt leaped up and gave her niece a hug. "Megan, it is good you are

here," she whispered, so as not to wake Gabriel.

Megan kept her voice low also. "Of course. I came as soon as I could."

Her uncle greeted her warmly also. "We are so thankful you could come. Your father will have the surgery tomorrow morning."

"Yes, the nurse told me over the phone."

Gabriel Vasquez heard his daughter's voice and peeked his eyes open. "*Mija*, is that you?"

Megan ran to his side. "Yes, it's me, Dad," she clutched his hand.

"How are you, baby girl?"

She squeezed back tears. "I'm good, Dad. How are *you*?"

"Eh, I could be better. But at least I'm alive!"

His comment made Megan chuckle in spite of the flood threatening to overflow from her eyes. His brother and sister-in-law slipped out of the room to give them some privacy.

"They're going to cut me open tomorrow, fix up this ol' ticker of mine," Gabriel said.

"So I heard!" Megan squeezed his hand harder.

Her dad patted the hand that held his. "It's gonna be fine, *Mija*. I'm tough. I don't plan on meeting our Heavenly Father just yet."

"I'm not sure that's something you get a say in," Megan raised one eyebrow.

Mr. Vasquez shrugged. "If that's the case, so be it. But I'm not going to worry about that going in, and you shouldn't either."

"You know I'm going to be praying for you anyways," Megan said.

"And I appreciate that," he smiled.

A nurse entered the room and told Megan that she needed to leave while some tests were being administered on her father.

"I'll see you in a bit, Dad," she told her father. He nodded, and she left the room.

She found her *tío* and *tía* in the family waiting room, getting some coffee. A strong cup sounded good to her too. The coffee wasn't nearly as good as that from Enchanted Moon or Dominican Java, but it was enough to revive her energy.

Victoria patted the sofa beside her, and Megan accepted the invitation to sit.

"So, *mi sobrina*, your father tells me you have a new boyfriend," Victoria's eyes twinkled.

Megan sighed. "Oh. Well...things didn't exactly work out with him, I'm sorry to say."

Victoria's smile turned to a frown of sympathy. "I am so sorry to hear that. Are you okay?"

For the millionth time that weekend, it seemed, Megan's eyes filled with tears. "Yeah," she choked. Her aunt pulled her into a hug, sending Megan past the point of control. Tears streamed down her face as she began to sob. Her uncle leaned over from his seat and patted her knee. "It's gonna be alright, Megan," he tried to reassure her.

"Do you want to talk about it?" her aunt offered.

Megan spilled her guts, telling them every detail about what had happened with Levi.

Her *Tío* Miguel shook his head. "That *malo* did a bad thing, two-timing you! Why do you keep falling in love with these *pendejo*, these...these rascals, these... jerks!" He struggled to find the right English word.

But Victoria was not convinced that Levi was such a jerk. "Are you sure about what you saw, Megan? This girl, is she really his girlfriend?"

"She kept going on and on about her boyfriend at the party. Then when Levi showed up, she said 'here he is now', and ran over to give him a big kiss."

"But what does this Levi say about it?" Victoria pressed. "Have you talked to him?"

Megan shook her head. "No, I haven't."

"Then how do you know she is telling the truth?"

Megan gulped. "He said that they broke up a while ago," she admitted.

"See? Maybe she is the one lying, not him," Victoria pointed out.

"But I found a picture of them together in his car. If they broke up, why did he keep it? Also, just after she came back to Austin, he kept getting text messages from somebody during our date and was distracted by it the whole evening. I bet anything the messages were from her."

"You cannot make that assumption. Besides, even if they were from her, it does not prove that he was cheating on you. Perhaps she is some crazy stalker-person," Victoria suggested.

Miguel nodded. "It does seem like that could be a possibility."

"My friend did say that Renee is kind of a *loca*--she does a lot of crazy things. They used to be roommates, before she went abroad."

"Why don't you call this boy, ask him to tell you the truth?"

"I can't."

"Why not?"

"Because I blocked his number and deleted it from my phone," Megan squeezed her eyes shut. Man, she was really regretting that choice now!

"So, call his work instead," her aunt nodded firmly.

It's a good suggestion, Megan thought. But she wasn't sure she had the guts to do it. Memories of finding the text messages on Brad's phone, of seeing him and Kimberly together, still seared her mind and made her chest hurt like a bad case of heartburn.

"I want to trust him, but I don't know if I can."

"Your heart will tell you what to do," Victoria squeezed Megan's hand.

Her aunt and uncle took her back to their house for a few hours so she could rest. Then they drove her over to the hospital again first thing in the morning. Megan decided that she had no time or energy to worry about calling Levi right then. She needed to focus all her energy on her dad, making sure he came out of this OK, and helping him to get back on his feet afterwards.

Her dad seemed bright and chipper, wearing a blue cap over his hair as the nurses prepared him for surgery.
"I got my chest hair shaved this morning," he grinned. "I look like one of those hairless Abercrombie models you used to idolize in High School."
"Dad!" Megan burst out laughing. For a brief time, she had indulged in putting up the giant posters of hunky models that she'd gotten in a store giveaway, a detail her Dad apparently hadn't forgotten.
Megan held his hand again. "I'm going to be here the whole time you know, with *Tío* Miguel and *Tía* Victoria. When you get done, we'll come see you as soon as they let us."
"I know, *Mija*. I'm gonna be fine, you'll see. See you in a few hours."
Megan nodded, determined she wouldn't cry again. Not in front of her dad, at least.

She passed her aunt and uncle in the hall.
"We are going to the cafeteria to get some food, if you would like to join us," they invited.
"Thanks, but I think I'll go to the chapel for a while to pray," she told them.
"Of course," Victoria said. "We will come later to pray also."

There were a few others praying in the chapel when Megan entered. A few wooden pews faced a small altar, above which a crucifix was hung. The sole window in the room was a lovely stained-glass piece that stretched the full length from ceiling to floor. Megan took a seat in one of the pews and began to pray.
Someone's cell phone began to ring. The woman in front of Megan glared at the owner as he frantically tried to silence it.
"No cell phones," she hissed, pointing to a sign on the wall. The woman returned to praying as the man turned off his ringer entirely. Megan followed suit, not wanting her own phone to be the next source of disturbance to anyone's spiritual conversations.
She turned her attention back to God, and spent the next hour praying for her father.

Meanwhile, back in Austin, Levi was still struggling to get a hold of Megan. Trips to her apartment had proved futile, and he had given up hoping that she might answer her phone or any of his texts. He couldn't get rid of the ache in his heart though.
His colleagues noticed his somber demeanor.
"Trouble in the love department?" Bart asked.
Levi told him the jist of what had happened, and how he couldn't reach her to try to explain.

"Why don't you just go by her work and see if she's there?" Bart suggested. Levi took his advice. As soon as his shift was over, he went to Hobby Lobby. Considering it was a weekday afternoon, he expected to find her there. But her former co-workers told him she'd been laid off the day before.
Great timing, he thought. He checked the coffee shop next.

Sierra and Patrice were both working at the counter when he entered. Levi was surprised to see the two of them working, with neither Megan, nor Duke, nor even Keenan in sight.
"Witty," Patrice called him when she saw him. He frowned. "Sorry," she apologized. "Old habits die hard. Levi, surprised to see you here."
"I'm looking for Megan, is she here?"
Sierra shook her head. "She had a family emergency," she explained. "She left yesterday to fly back to Santa Fe."
Levi let out a loud whistle. "She has *not* had a great weekend, has she?"
"No thanks to you," Sierra pointed out.
"You mean, no thanks to Renee!" Patrice jumped in.
"Thank you!" Levi exclaimed. "You know, that wasn't me, that was all her back at the party, right?"
"You're really not still together with her then, huh?" Sierra asked.
"No way! We broke up months ago when she left for France. But that psycho somehow thinks that we were still in a long-distance relationship and that she could just pick up where we left off coming back. Patrice, she was your roommate-- you know she's nuts!"
Patrice nodded her head vigorously. "Nuttier than a peanut-butter factory!"
"Look, I'll show you proof that we're not together." He thumbed through Renee's Facebook profile, which was littered with photos of her hanging all over a series of French men, even kissing some of them. "Even if I hadn't broken up with her, do you really think I would stay with her after she's behaved like this?"
The evidence was undeniable.
"Will you tell her to return my calls?" Levi asked.
"She deleted your number from her phone," Sierra said.
"Then give it to her again, please," he begged.
"I'll do you one better," Sierra offered. She pulled out her own phone and handed it to him. "Hers is at the top of the favorites list," she said.

Levi paced the floor nervously while he waited for Megan to answer. But she never picked up. He hung up the phone.
"What should I do? It just went to voicemail."
"Try her again!" Patrice urged. "And this time, leave a message if she doesn't pick up."
Once again, Megan's voicemail picked up the call, but this time, Levi did as Patrice suggested.

"Hey, Megan, it's Levi. Sierra let me use her phone. Before you delete this, I just want you to know, I wasn't lying to you when I said I had broken up with Renee. I wasn't seeing her behind your back. I would never do that to you. When she came back, she started stalking me again, kept calling and texting me repeatedly asking to meet up, even though I'd told her I wasn't interested. She'd invited me to come to some party on New Year's Eve, but I turned her down. I had no idea it would end up being the same party you'd asked me to."
There was a bit of silence while Levi tried to figure out what to say next. Finally, he said, "Look, I know you might never be willing to give me another chance. But I just want you to know, from the moment you walked into my life, you're the only woman I've ever thought of. You're amazing, Megan Vasquez, and I'll never forget the time we spent together." Levi bit his lip to keep back the tide of his emotions from spilling over. "Anyways," he said at last, "goodbye. Oh wait, here's my number, in case you change your mind and want to call me." He quickly rattled off a series of digits. "Well that's that then. Bye."
He handed the phone back to Sierra, who promised to put in a good word for him the next time she talked to Megan.

At the hospital, Megan and her family waited anxiously for news of how Mr. Vasquez' surgery had gone. Megan's stomach was in such knots, she had no appetite, but her aunt finally pressed her to eat a sandwich from the cafeteria. Megan found a book in the waiting room, one which was supposed to be a bestseller, yet she had never read. She tried to keep herself occupied with it but found that after half an hour all she had done was continually re-read the first page. Her uncle busied himself with a game on his phone, while her aunt read a few magazines and filed her nails.
Eventually, Megan fell asleep on the waiting room sofa. Her aunt woke her when the nurse came in.
"Mr. Vasquez is out of surgery now. The operation was a success."
"Is he awake? Can I see him?" Megan asked.
"He's still asleep. We need to run some more tests on him, then after that, you all can see him." The nurse nodded, then left to tend to her patients.

Megan let out a huge sigh of relief.
"It is good news, Megan!" Victoria exclaimed.
"I will call the rest of the family to tell them," Miguel declared.
Megan nodded. "I should call Sierra. She's known me and my dad since high school. She'll want to know how he is."
"Of course," Victoria said.
Megan realized she had never switched her phone back on since turning it off in the chapel. To her surprise, there were two missed calls from Sierra and a voicemail. But this surprise was matched by a greater one when she listened to the message and realized it was from Levi, not Sierra. Two nights ago, she had been so angry with Levi, that she wouldn't even listen to his voicemails, she just

deleted them, then got so fed up that she'd blocked him from calling. Now, she was ready to listen to what he had to say.
Her eyes watered as she listened to Levi's explanation. It fit with what her friends had told her about Renee, and it fit with what she had known of Levi's character up to that point. If he was lying in order to keep stringing her along, he was doing a darn good job of it, she had to conclude. The more logical assumption was that he was telling the truth; Renee had no part in his life anymore, despite her pitiful attempts to be.

Megan wiped the liquid pooling in her eyes. She remembered the purpose for which she had turned on her phone, to communicate the news about her dad's surgery to Sierra. This was expediently done. After expressing her relief about Mr. Vasquez' condition, Sierra mentioned that Levi had come into the coffee shop earlier.
"Yes, I listened to his voicemail," Megan told her.
"And?" Sierra questioned.
"And what?" Megan replied.
"Are you going to forgive him and get back together?"
The nurse reentered the room to give them an update.
"I've gotta go. I'll call you again later, okay?" Megan hastily said.
"K, bye, *Chica*!"

"Your dad just woke up," the nurse told her. "You can go in to see him now." Megan followed the nurse down the hall to her dad's room. Mr. Vasquez was still groggy, but he was glad to see Megan.
"I told you, *Mija*, your dad is strong!" he said to her.
"I know you are, Dad." She sat by his side for a bit. Miguel and Victoria joined them soon.
"If you're up for it, there's some more company here to see you," Miguel told his brother.
Gabriel nodded, and Miguel admitted their youngest brother Luis and his wife, Teresa. Luis was the other brother who lived in the area. They had two more brothers who lived in Colorado, and a sister who lived in Arizona.
Gabriel was happy to see Luis. "I'm so glad you could come."
"Of course," Luis said. "Teresa and I came as soon as we got off work."
They visited until the doctor entered. He was surprised to see so many people in the room.
"Wow, it's good to see you have so many visitors, Gabriel!"
Gabriel chuckled. "You should see how many of us there are at family dinners!"
"I came to give you an update," Dr. Rampal said. "Your tests all came back normal, and everything is looking good after your surgery."
"That's great," Mr. Vasquez nodded. "When do I get to go home?"
Dr. Rampal adjusted his glasses on his face. "Well, let's see. Today's Monday. If your condition remains stable and there are no complications, you will be

released on Thursday."

"Wonderful!"

Megan had moved close to the door to allow her uncles time with their brother. As the doctor turned to exit, he addressed her.

"Ms. Vasquez, right?" They had spoken once before the surgery and he remembered her as being the patient's daughter.

She nodded.

"May I speak with you in the hall about something?"

Megan knew it must be something serious if he wanted to talk to her alone. With trepidation filling her heart, she followed Dr. Rampal into the hall.

Chapter 12

Dr. Rampal began, "your father's surgery was a success, as you know. We were able to restore his heart up to ninety-five percent of its original function, and we ended up putting three stents in, not two, as we had originally planned."
"But…" Megan urged at the hesitation in his voice.
"Ms. Vasquez, I'll be frank with you. Your father has a long recovery ahead of him. It will be a couple of weeks before he can drive again, and still longer before he can return to work. He will need a lot of care, especially in the early weeks of his recovery. I see that you have a lot of family nearby. Is there anyone who would be able to assist with his care?"
Megan thought for a minute. Luis and Teresa were both in their thirties; they each worked, and they had four school-age children to care for besides. Miguel and Victoria's children were all grown, but they both had full-time jobs as well. They had taken time off to be near Gabriel during his surgery, but she doubted that they had enough vacation time to care for him in the upcoming weeks. Their other siblings all lived too far away to be of any assistance.
She realized who it had to be.
"I'll do it," she said. "I can stay home with my father to care for him as long as he needs."
"I'm relieved to hear it," Dr. Rampal smiled. He nodded as he continued down the hall to other patients.

It was getting late and everyone was hungry. Victoria did not fancy another meal in the hospital cafeteria. She got on the phone with her son and daughters, and within half an hour, they had said "goodnight" to Gabriel, and everyone, including Megan, set out to meet the rest of the family at a local restaurant for dinner.
Victoria had chosen a popular Mexican restaurant not far from the hospital, and that their family frequented. Megan rode with Miguel and Victoria. Luis and Teresa had to make a side-trip to pick their kids up from the neighbor who was watching them and would be late to the restaurant.
Megan's cousins arrived at the restaurant shortly after they did, and their party was seated, taking up most of the patio over four large tables. They numbered twenty-two in all; Miguel and Victoria had four children, two of whom were married. There were four grandsons and three granddaughters from these marriages, plus Luis and Teresa's children, which made it so that the children equaled the adults in number. Megan happily found herself seated between Miguel and Victoria's two youngest daughters Carolina and Estella, both who were still single and close in age to herself. With so much family around, Megan

had little time to continue thinking about Levi. It had been months since she had seen her aunts and uncles or any of her cousins, and they all wanted to catch up with her. Carolina was now a student at Megan's alma mater, so of course she had to share all the latest news about what was happening around campus and how their football team had fared that year. Her sister, Estella, was studying at New Mexico State, U of NM's biggest rival, so she felt compelled to make some jokes about how poorly her sister and cousin's school had done compared to the success of NMSU's team. Megan enjoyed the banter, though she cared little for football herself.

Megan returned to her aunt and uncle's house to spend the night again. Her cousins wanted to stay up late since they were home on winter break, so they put a movie on in the living room. Megan slipped away to the guest room. She still hadn't returned Levi's call yet. Her situation had changed so much since leaving Austin, she hardly knew what to say. She fumbled in her purse until she found the scrap of napkin that she'd jotted his number down on. Bucking up her courage, she dialed the number and waited for Levi to pick up.
"Hullo?" he answered groggily on the fourth ring.
"Oh! Darn, I forgot about the time change, sorry," Megan apologized.
"Megan, is that you?" Levi asked.
"Yeah, it's me," she said.
"It's good to hear your voice," he said. "So, listen, I--"
"I know, Levi," Megan interrupted him. "I heard your message earlier, and I get it. I'm sorry I overreacted when I saw Renee kiss you."
"Hey, I totally get it," Levi said. "I probably would have flipped out too, if I had seen the same thing happen with you and Brad. Sorry," he said, realizing he'd probably brought up a sore subject.
"I believe you when you say you had nothing to do with her kissing you."
"She's totally crazy!" Levi exclaimed. "Even after the party, when I told her in no uncertain terms that we were finished, she still drunk called me in the middle of the night. Twice, no less. And she showed up to my work today, if you can believe it, begging and pleading with me to give her another chance. She got so out of hand, that Bart had to have her escorted off the property."
Megan whistled. "Dang!"

Levi took a deep breath. "So, uh, now that that whole misunderstanding is cleared up, I was wondering, where do you and I stand?"
Megan paused. This next part would be painful, she knew. "Look, Levi, I'm not mad anymore, now that I know what really happened. The thing is, my dad is going to need some help for a while as he's recovering."
"How's he doing, by the way?"
"He's great! Thanks for asking. The surgery was a complete success."
"I'm so glad to hear that."
"Anyways, the doctors said it's going to be several weeks before he can return to

work, and in the meantime, he will need someone to look after him. I'm planning to stay here in Santa Fe to be that someone."
"That's great! We can talk over the phone or do video calls until you get back--" Levi began, but Megan interrupted him again.
"Look, Levi, I'm not going to lead you on. The time we spent together was wonderful. You made me feel so special, and I'll never forget the wonderful Christmas we spent with your family. But right now, my future is very uncertain, and my dad needs all my attention. I think it would be better if we don't try to pursue anything further between us right now."
"I don't understand. I thought things were going so well between us," Levi said.
"They were!"
"Then what's the problem? I thought once the misunderstanding between us was cleared, we could pick up where we left off. Albeit a slight delay, with you staying to help your dad for a while."
"That's just it though, it might be more than a while."
"That's okay, you can take all the time you want. I'll be here," Levi assured her.
"No, Levi, you don't get it," Megan tried not to cry. "I don't want us to get back together."
Levi was stunned. When he found his voice again, he said, "you're right. I don't get it!"
"You're mad now, aren't you?"
"Yeah! I mean, a little," Levi admitted. "Mostly just confused. Why would you give up on us just when we had found each other? You know, you're like Xu Bing's books; I keep trying to read you, but it's like you're written in a language that no man can understand."
"I don't know when I'll be back," Megan repeated.
"Yeah, and that's fine!"
"I might not even be coming back. I might stay here permanently."
"For good? You're not coming back at all?" Levi felt his mouth run dry.
"I really don't know. I mean, my stuff is still there, so I suppose I'll have to make a trip back at some point to move it or else hire someone to help me, but yeah, I have no idea when I'll be back to Austin, if ever."
Levi's heart was broken. It took him a minute to regain his composure enough that he could disguise the swelling sobs in his throat.
 "Well, friends, at least?" he finally managed.
"Sure. Friends," Megan repeated.
"Okay," Levi conceded. "Don't be a stranger then. Friend." His voice was hollow. He hung up the phone. Megan felt an emptiness in her heart. *It's for the best*, she told herself.

By Thursday morning, Mr. Vasquez was well enough to be discharged, and Megan brought him back to the home she'd shared with him before moving to Austin. Her room was still exactly the same, minus the Abercrombie posters. It was right across the hall from her dad's room, meaning she could hear him if he needed any help during the night. Her aunts and cousins frequently came by with meals, so she hardly had to cook at all the first few weeks.

Megan was worried that with her dad out of work and she also, they wouldn't have money to pay the bills, including the rent on her apartment back in Austin, where most of her stuff was still at. She was pleasantly surprised to learn that her dad had a decent amount of savings, and that with the exception of their water and electricity, he had paid all the bills in advance for the next six months in order to get the discounts that came with doing so, and there was plenty left to cover her vacant apartment for as long as she needed.
"Comes with being a life-long saver and penny-pincher," he said.

Megan had been living with her dad for a full month before she began to think about getting a job. She brushed up her resume and applied to a few jobs in data analysis.
"Why don't you try calling up your old company to see if they have anything?" Her dad suggested. To her surprise, they were eager to take her back. The replacement they'd hired when she left hadn't worked out so good and had just left them to go to a rival company. But there was a condition: they wanted her to work at their new Austin office.
Megan told them she had to think about it.

Her father didn't see the problem with it.
"I worked hard all my life, and so did your grandparents, in order to ensure that you grew up well, had a college education, and were able to make a career for yourself after graduation. I hate to see you throw a great opportunity away, just because of where the job is at," he told her.
"I know, Dad. I'm just not sure that I want to go back there again," Megan told him. "Living there, it hasn't been the greatest experience for me, you know. Plus, I have to think about taking care of you, now."
"I understand, *Mija*," Gabriel nodded. "But you know, I've been thinking for a while now about where I'd like to retire."
"Retire? Aren't you going back to work after you get better?"
"I thought about that. I'm getting up there in years--"
"You are NOT old, Dad!"
"I know," he laughed, "but I'm old enough that working in the construction industry is tough on me. I've been saving up my retirement money for a long time, as you probably figured out when you saw my accounts. I think it might be time for me to hang up the ol' hard hat, enjoy my golden years. I've been doing some research online, and there are some nice retirement communities in Georgetown, just a little way outside of Austin."
"So, what you're saying is, you want to retire in Austin?" Megan asked.
"Well, only if you're going to be there!" Mr. Vasquez smiled. "Last time, you moved to Austin for the wrong reasons. Maybe this time you can go back for the

right ones."

Megan nodded. "But what about all of our family? Miguel and Victoria and Luis and Teresa, and all the rest of them?"

Gabriel shrugged. "They'll do just fine without me, I'm sure. They all have their children and grandchildren to mind. Me, I just have you to look out for. It's your decision where you'd like to live, have your career, but if you're amenable to it, I'd love it if I could live close by to wherever that might be."

"Oh, Dad!" A teary-eyed Megan threw her arms around his neck.

The opportunity to work for her old company again was a good one, Megan knew. So, another month later, when Mr. Vasquez was well enough to travel, their family helped them pack up all his belongings and they hired a moving truck for the biggest stuff. After a tearful family gathering with all the aunts, uncles, and cousins at Miguel and Victoria's house, Megan drove her dad in his beat-up Ford pickup all the way from Santa Fe to Austin.

They stayed the first night in her old apartment. She'd left in such a big hurry, there had been no time to clean out the fridge or do anything. She found some nasty leftovers in the back of the fridge that had enough mold to pass for a grade-school science experiment and some produce in the drawers that had gone rotten. Most of the pantry goods and stuff in the freezer was still OK, so there was enough for her to whip up a quick supper. While the food was heating up, Megan tried to straighten up the place.

"I'm sorry it's such a mess here, Dad!" she apologized as she ran around putting misplaced articles in their homes and gathering old mail for the trash can. As she moved some papers and books off an end table, she found a book that wasn't part of her collection. In fact, she remembered checking it out the last time she went to the library, but she never got to read it, and apparently, never returned it either.

"Oh gosh, I wonder what the library fine on this one's going to be?" she groaned.

Her dad saw the book in her hands. "Is that from *the* library?" his eyes twinkled.

"Dad…" Megan began in a scolding tone of voice. "Don't get any ideas!"

"Oh, I'm not. It's just that, well, suppose you go to return the book and *he* happens to be there. What will you say to him?"

Megan sucked in her breath. Despite parting on good terms with Levi, she hadn't spoken to him at all the past two months. She wondered if he'd forgotten about her by now. It had been twice as long as the time they dated since they had seen each other. Maybe he had already moved on to someone else. She voiced these thoughts to her dad.

"You won't know unless you talk to him. Do you want to talk to him?" he asked.

Megan sank onto the couch. "I mean, I don't know," she was quaking. "I shut that door pretty firmly the last time we talked."

"Doors can open as well as shut," Gabriel gently reminded her. "It's up to you whether or not you want them to." He put his arm around Megan. "Look, I know you've been hurt pretty bad in the past. But I know back in December when you were with Levi, you were like a different person. You had your lively spirit back. You seemed happy again, maybe even the happiest I'd ever seen you. Every time we called each other, you had good things to say about Levi, about all the wonderful things you were doing together, about how great his family is, about all the lovely staff at the library that you were making friends with."

"You know, I have to say this," Gabriel looked her right in the eyes. "The whole time you were with that Brad fellow, you never really seemed happy. You would say that things were going fine, but every time I looked into your eyes or heard your voice, there was this element of sadness or discomfort. I never had the misfortune to meet Brad in person, but there were a couple of times I didn't like the way he treated you. Like that time that he stood you up and you waited the whole evening at that restaurant without so much as a phone call from him. Or that time that he promised to bring you to that free concert in the park you wanted so much to go to, and then at the last minute he changed plans and said he wanted to go to a basketball game instead."

"I told you, he got free tickets from a friend for that," Megan argued.

"Yes, but that's not the point I'm making," her dad said. "He always seemed to be putting himself first, not you, and doing things that disrespected you or made you feel bad. And you always came up with excuses for him."

Megan's eyes were teary again. "You're not wrong, Dad."

"When you said you and Brad wanted to get engaged so you could live together, I wasn't really in favor of it, but I didn't want to stand in your way. I permitted it, but I never truly gave my blessing."

Shame filled Megan, as she remembered the reckless way that she had followed Brad to Austin and insisted that they get engaged.

Mr. Vasquez continued. "When you found out that that man was cheating on you, it broke my heart, *Mija*, it broke me so hard to see you so hurt!"

Megan couldn't even reply, she was so full of emotion.

"I know you had a misunderstanding with this Levi boy, but I hope my dear, that as you have resolved that, you might consider what Levi means to you now, if he means anything."

Megan shrugged. "You always did tell me, 'there are lots of fish in the sea'," she managed to say.

Gabriel nodded. "That's true, I did say that. But it's also true that not all fish in the sea are the same. Men like Levi, they don't come around every day. So, the question is, do you want to go hunting again for that fish that got away?"

Megan looked at the book still in her hands. A flood of memories surged in her mind, memories she had shared with Levi. They raced along like a movie playing backwards in her head, starting with the horrible encounter New Year's

Eve, to the perfect Christmas in Spring, TX, to their dates at the Museum of the Weird, the Trail of Lights, the coffee shops, all the times they spent at the library, the chance encounter at the Blanton followed by ice cream, all the way up to their first meeting at the library, when she had thought he was so nice and so handsome, and he had helped her find her favorite book.

In that instant, she knew that she had to take a chance, she had to see if Levi still cared about her. Her dad saw it on her face without her even saying it aloud.
"Go to him, *Mija*, he urged."
"What about you?"
"I'll be fine here, get going!"
Dinner lay in the microwave, forgotten for the time being. In the time it took Megan to slip her shoes on, she was out the door, library book in hand. She jumped in her dad's old pickup and sped off. It only took a few minutes to reach the library. Megan parked the truck and tried to calm her nerves.
It's okay, you can do this, she told herself. She wiped her sweaty palms on her jeans.

Walking through the familiar automatic doors of Yarborough Library, she expected to see Levi shelving books, just like she had the first day they'd met. But he was nowhere in sight.
Well, this is anticlimactic, Megan thought.
Loretta spotted her right away. "Well I'll be! Ain't you a sight for sore eyes!" she exclaimed. "Megan, honey, how've you been?" She stood from her counter and waddled over to give Megan a bear-hug.
"I'm good, Loretta."
"Are you just back to visit, or--"
"I'm back for good now," Megan smiled. "Oh," she handed her the library book she'd been holding, "I'm a little afraid to find out how much the fine will be for this overdue book!"
Loretta chuckled. "Honey, for you, I think we can make an exception and waive the fee. Levi told me what you'd been through, with your dad and everything."
"Speaking of Levi, where is he? I thought he'd be working today."
"Not today, Honey, sorry," Loretta apologized.
Bart walked past. He also said "hello" to Megan, and indicated how happy he was, or rather, how happy *someone* would be, to have her back.
But he's not here right now, Megan thought.
Loretta discerned the look on Megan's face. "You know," she said, "you could always call him."
Of course, Megan chided herself, *that would be the logical thing to do. I don't know why I expected this to play out like a movie!*

She promised Loretta that she would visit again soon. Then Megan drove home. As she passed by the park across from her apartment, she noticed someone

sitting on the bench that directly faced her home. It was Levi! Her heart began to pound at an alarming rate. She parked the truck in front of her apartment. Checking for traffic, she crossed the street. Levi had to be waiting for *her*-- he had to! Seeing her approach, he stood up from the bench, a smile slowly spreading across his face.
"Hi," he said.
"Hi," Megan replied awkwardly. "How-- how did you know to come here?" Megan asked him.
"Sierra phoned me to say you were moving back, and that you'd be arriving today. I went by your place first and met your dad there. He told me you'd gone to the library to find me. I figured this would be a good spot to wait for you to come back," he grinned. "Wanna take a stroll?"
Megan nodded. They began down the same pathway where they'd shared their first kiss.

"So, how've you been?" Levi asked.
"I'm good," Megan answered. She told him about getting rehired by her old company, but at their new Austin office. He inquired about her dad's health, which she was happy to inform him was improving every day. She asked Levi how he was doing also.
"I took your suggestion," was what he said.
"Which one?"
"I went back to school. I'm finishing my bachelor's, but in sociology, with a minor in classic literature, instead of majoring in art."
"Classic literature?" Megan raised an eyebrow.
Levi chuckled. "Yeah, I surprised myself with that one. Turns out I love all those classics that you adore. I've read all Jane Austen's books since you left-- and not just the quirky variations. The real deal. I've been reading Gaskell, Dickens, the Brontës, Trollope-- all the authors you love, and many more. Our professor has us reading *Les Misérables* right now, which I must say, is an amazing book!"
"Isn't it?" Megan agreed. "I just finished the one you recommended to me by Andy Weir-- *The Martian*. I got sucked into the *Emperor's Edge* series as well."
"Oh yeah, by Lindsay Buroker?" Levi asked.
Megan nodded. "Yep."
"I loved those. Seems we've influenced each other's taste in books," he pointed out.
"Yeah," Megan said softly. Her heart was brimming up with all the things she wanted to say to Levi, but she didn't know how to begin.

They reached the exact spot where Levi had first kissed her. Megan knew it was, because she recognized the statue of the little girl chasing a butterfly. Levi took Megan's hands and turned her to face him.
"There's something I've been wanting to say to you," he began.
"Yeah, me too," Megan nodded.

"Ever since you left-- no, ever since the first day I met you, I haven't been able to get you off my mind. When you said you just wanted to be friends, I tried to forget you, but you just stuck there like glue. The truth is, I started reading all those classics because I wanted to still feel a connection to you. Then I fell in love with the books themselves, so I added literature to my degree!" he laughed.
"So, now you love the books instead of me?" Megan teased.
Levi shook his head, still chuckling. "No. The books did nothing to diminish my feelings for you. In fact, they only increased it. Megan, you are, without a doubt the most amazing woman I have ever met. You're kind, beautiful, smart, fun to be around, great taste in art, music, and books."
Megan let out a small laugh, a blush quickly spreading across her cheeks.
Levi went on, "The thing is, I don't want us to just be friends. I know we had some miscommunication. Things didn't go down well the last time we saw each other--"
"Oh, don't even bring that up!" Megan interrupted. "I was so foolish to not even give you a chance to explain before I rushed off like that. I should have given you the benefit of the doubt. I should have known better than to think that…"
Levi nodded. "That I was like Brad," he finished her sentence. "Trust me, I get it. You got hurt before. Bad. And that made it hard for you to trust me. I should have told you that Renee was still stalking me."
Megan kept her head down in shame. "I get why you didn't."
Levi gently lifted her chin so he could look into her lustrous brown eyes. "So, what do you say, Megan Vasquez? Will you give me another chance? Can we try again?"
A smile spread across Megan's face. "Yes," she nodded. "I'd like that very much!"
She melted into Levi's embrace. His sweet lips felt familiar, like coming home after a long trip. Resting in his arms, Megan felt safe and loved.
This is where she belonged.

Chapter 13

Two years later

Megan folded up her laptop and packed it in her pretty computer bag that had a Monet painting printed on it-- a birthday gift from Sierra. *Thank goodness it's Friday,* she thought to herself. Walking down the hall of the North Austin office building where she worked, she wished her co-workers a good weekend, waving at them in their cubicles as she passed by. Her phone chirped just as she stepped off the elevator. She answered it, walking to her car in the parking lot as she talked.
"Hey there, Mister."
"Hey there, Beautiful," Levi replied. Hearing his deep mellow voice made a smile spread across Megan's face. Levi continued, "are you on your way?"
"Yeah, just got off work. I'm getting in my car now." Levi and Megan were planning to meet at Enchanted Moon, where their friends would be celebrating Sierra's promotion to Curator of Modern Art at the Blanton Art Museum. Her degree had paid off; following her graduation from the master's program, she'd been hired on as a gallery assistant at the Blanton, and now, nearly two years later, she was getting the job of her dreams.
"Hey, would you mind swinging by the library?" Levi asked. "I forgot something at work."
"Sure thing. Just text me the details," Megan agreed.
"Will do." They said goodbye, and Megan made a slight detour on her route south to drop by the library. Before she got there, she heard the text from Levi come through. It was a call number for a book in the fiction section. Nothing else was said about it.
"Huh, that's funny," Megan thought aloud.

"Megan, Honey, how ya' doin'?" Loretta lumbered from her chair to give Megan a hug when she entered the building.
"I'm good, Loretta," Megan answered as the older woman squeezed her so hard, she thought her ribs might crack. "I'm just here to pick up something for Levi."
"Go right ahead, don't let me stop you." Loretta grinned as if she knew something Megan didn't.
Ignoring that vibe, Megan went to the section as directed by the call number. She recognized the shelf. It was where the classics were kept, namely, where her favorite Jane Austen books were. A chuckle escaped Megan's lips when she realized what book matched the call numbers: *Pride and Prejudice.*
He knows I already have this one, Megan thought. *He bought it for me, in fact. What is*

going on here?
Megan's phone chimed, as if to answer on cue.
Check out page 221 of Chapter 34, third line. Read it aloud.
Megan's eyes narrowed. She looked around her, but the only other people nearby were some library visitors.
Obliging, she followed Levi's instructions. On page 221, she read Mr. Darcy's famous quote, "In vain have I struggled. It will not do. My feelings will not be repressed. You must allow me to tell you how ardently I admire and love you."
"And I do love you, most ardently," a familiar voice spoke behind Megan. She turned to face Levi, who must have been hiding somewhere nearby, but was now on his knees before her. Megan gasped. In his outstretched hands, he held an open jewelry box upon which sat a glittering diamond ring. Megan, speechless for the moment, allowed her lover to profess to her.
"I know I'm no 'Mr. Darcy'," Levi began, "but I believe my feelings for you can be no less than his were for Elizabeth Bennet."
Megan's eyes began to tear up.
"Megan Vasquez," he continued, "since I've known you, you've brought so much joy to me. Every day, I'm so thankful to have you in my life, and I wondered," he pulled the ring from its cushion and placed it on Megan's hand, "if you would do me the great honor of becoming my wife."
Tears of joy continued to roll down Megan's cheeks. "Yes!" she exclaimed. "A thousand times, yes!"
Levi got to his feet and Megan leaped into his arms. He spun her around and around as they both laughed. Finally setting her back on her feet, he brought his lips to Megan's in the kind of kiss that exploded like a firework show on the Fourth of July.

As the happy couple emerged from the rows of bookshelves, the entire library staff was waiting for them in the lobby. They erupted in a chorus of applause. Other library patrons cheered also.
Megan laughed again, wiping the dampness from her eyes with the sleeve of her jacket.
"Congratulations, Levi and Megan!" Bart spoke for all of them.
"I guess you guys knew that Levi had planned this," Megan grinned.
"You better believe it, Honey," Loretta chortled.
Levi pulled Megan into a side hug. "I had it planned all down to the wire, but I couldn't have pulled it off without all of you."
Megan and Levi accepted the hugs and hearty handshakes from each of their friends.
"Now if you'll excuse us," Levi said, "we've got a party to get to." They said goodbye and headed out in Megan's car.

"You know, you're wrong about something," Megan remarked.
"What's that?" Levi asked.

"I think you are a 'Mr. Darcy' kind of guy; at least, to me, you are!"
Levi laughed. "Thanks, Megs, although personally, I think I see myself more as that funny guy from *Northanger Abbey*."
"Mr. Tilney, you mean?"
"That's the one! Great sense of humor, knows about muslin."
Megan giggled. "What do you know about muslin?"
"Not a lot, actually," Levi admitted. "But the guy was on point when it came to reading. 'The person, be it gentleman or lady, who has not pleasure in a good novel, must be intolerably stupid'," he quoted.
"I'm impressed!" Megan approved.
"Yes, my dear, I have finally succeeded."
"In what?"
"In becoming an Austenite Austinite!" Levi quipped.
Megan burst into another fit of laughter.

They pulled into the parking lot of Enchanted Moon.
"Let's not say anything right away," Megan said. "I don't want our news to steal Sierra's thunder."
"Sure," Levi smiled. But Megan was in for another surprise. As soon as they walked in, the party assembled shouted in unison, "Congratulations!"
Duke pulled a string, and a shower of balloons rained down on them from the ceiling.
With mirth, Megan asked, "how did you all know already?"
Sierra hurried over to hug Megan. "Oh, you know, Levi might have texted us on the way."
"But this was already planned," Megan pointed out. She looked from Sierra to the sheepish grin on Levi's face.
He shrugged. "I had a pretty good idea that you would say 'yes'," he admitted.
"Aww, you guys are the best!" Megan exclaimed. Patrice and Duke, who were next closest in proximity, gave Megan their hugs also.

Patrice was now Duke's manager for the Enchanted Moon; after graduating in art, she decided she really preferred working at the coffee shop, at least until she could make a living off of her paintings and drawings. The coffee shop, once adorned with photos of jazz singers, had now become a gallery for Patrice's work. The photo of Duke Ellington was still in its prominent place though.

For Duke, business was doing so well, he'd decided to open up two more locations in other parts of town. He'd hired the analytics company where Megan worked to help him research the best spots to expand his enterprise. Work would begin soon to renovate a strip mall location not far from Megan's office, and a new construction site was ongoing downtown for a large shopping area in which Duke had already secured a unit.

Megan's dad was also at the party. Unknown to her, Levi had visited Gabriel Vasquez a few days prior to obtain his blessing for marrying Megan. Gabriel had told him that nothing would make him happier than to see the two wed. Retirement suited Gabriel. He was thriving in the Sun City community where his townhouse lay. He had made a large number of friends, found a wonderful church close enough that he could walk to, and had brushed up on his high-school trumpet skills enough to join a local mariachi band.
"I'm so happy for you, *Mija*," he told Megan as he pulled her into a bear-hug.
"Thanks, Dad," Megan said, returning the embrace.

Levi and Megan's friends from the library were not far behind. They joined the party in time to enjoy the cake and refreshments that Duke had prepared for everyone.

Sierra was right behind Megan in line to get a slice of the cake. Megan glanced at her.
"I thought this party was supposed to be in *your* honor, not mine."
"Pff," Sierra waved, "when have I ever needed a party to be about me? That was just a ruse we created to get you to come."
Megan raised one brow, "but you did get the promotion at work, didn't you?"
"Of course!" Sierra laughed.
"Good, because the directors at the Blanton would be fools not to recognize your talent."

Megan and Levi stayed until the end of the party. While Duke and Patrice cleaned up and closed up the shop, Jimmy Dean's song, "My Heart is an Open Book", came on the playlist. Megan remembered it as one of the ones they'd sung along with on the trip to Spring.
"Care to dance, Miss Vasquez?" Levi extended his hand to Megan.
"Soon to be 'Mrs. Whittaker'," she replied as she took his hand.
"I like the sound of that," Levi nodded, pulling her into his arms for a slow dance. He hummed along with the song.
"It's just like the song says: my heart is an open book," Levi told her. "I will always be true to you, and only you."
Megan smiled. "I know. I love you, Levi Whittaker," she told him.
"I love you too, Megan Vasquez."
"Forever and always."
"Forever and always," Levi repeated, before drawing his lips to hers in a tender kiss.

Acknowledgements

My gratitude goes out to the many people who helped me create this book. In particular, I would like to thank my cultural sensitivity readers: Mindi, Leigh, Danielle, Maria, and Laura. Your critical feedback helped me to better showcase Megan's Mexican heritage and avoid any major faux-pas.

A thanks also goes out to my wonderful beta readers: Nancy, Jenn, Sarah, Britaini, and Sabina. Thank you for sharing your thoughts to help me improve the overall story.

I'd also like to mention Emily Wittig, my incredibly talented graphic designer. Thank you for being able to discern my inner thoughts about what I wanted and bringing to life this spectacular cover. You really made Levi and Megan come to life on the front of my book!

Last, but certainly not least, I would like to thank my family: Moses, Alyssa, Henry, and Claire, for their enduring love and support. You put up with all my funny writer's antics and continue to encourage me to pursue my dreams.

About the Author

Amanda Kai's background in the performing arts drives her creative spirit. Prior to becoming an author, Amanda enjoyed a successful career as a professional harpist, and danced ballet for twenty years. Her love of storytelling, nurtured by a fondness for period dramas and classic literature, led her to begin writing Jane Austen variations and other historical and contemporary romances. When she's not diving into the realm of her imagination, Amanda lives out her own happily ever after in Leander, Texas, with her husband and three children.

Other books by Amanda Kai

Thank you for reading my book! I hope you enjoyed it. I invite you to submit your honest review at your preferred retailer, Goodreads or BookBub. Your assessment will help other people like you to find my book and know whether they might like to read it.

Like my work? Get a FREE COPY of my book, "Elizabeth's Secret Admirer: a Pride and Prejudice Novella" when you sign up for my newsletter. Scan the QR code below to get your free book!

Want to stay connected? Follow me on my Facebook page at
www.facebook.com/authoramandakai

Other titles by Amanda Kai

Marriage and Ministry: a Pride and Prejudice Novel- The continuing story of Charlotte Lucas and William Collins

Keys: a Marie Antoinette story- a romantic short-story about the real-life Dauphine of France and her prince, Dauphin Louis-Auguste.

Made in the USA
Monee, IL
23 December 2020